After Me
Comes the Flood

ALSO BY SARAH PERRY

Melmoth

The Essex Serpent

After Me Comes the Flood

A Novel

Sarah Perry

HARPER LARGE PRINT

An Imprint of HarperCollinsPublishers

For RDP

Who makes one little room an everywhere

And for Jenny

Who was always on my side

FIRST HARPER LARGE PRINT EDITION

Library of Congress Cataloging-in-Publication Data is available upon request.

ISBN 978-0-06-297903-2

20 21 22 23 24 LSC 10 9 8 7 6 5 4 3 2 1

Wednesday

I

I'm writing this in a stranger's room on a broken chair at an old school desk. The chair creaks if I move, and so I must keep very still. The lid of the desk is scored with symbols that might have been made by children or men, and at the bottom of the inkwell a beetle is lying on its back. Just now I thought I saw it move, but it's dry as a husk and must've died long before I came.

There's a lamp on the floor by my feet with painted moths on the paper shade. The bulb has a covering of dust thick as felt, and I daren't turn it on in case they see and come and find me again. There are two windows at my side, and a bright light at the end of the garden throws a pair of slanted panels on the wall. It makes this paper yellow, and the skin of my hands: they don't look as if they have anything to do with me, and it makes me wonder where mine are, and what they're doing. I've been listening for footsteps on the stairs or voices in the garden, but there's only the sound of a household keeping quiet. They gave me too much drink—there's a kind of buzzing in my ears and if I close my eyes they sting . . .

I've never kept a diary before—nothing ever happens to me worth the trouble of writing it down. But I hardly believe what happened today, or what I've done—I'm afraid that in a month's time I'll think it was all some foolish novel I read years ago when I was young and knew no better. I brought nothing with me, and found this notebook pushed to the back of the drawer in the desk where I sit now, hidden by newspapers buckled with damp. The paper smells dank and all the pages are empty except the last, where someone's written the same name on every line as if they were practicing a signature. It's a strange name and I know it though I can't remember why: EADWACER, EADWACER, EADWACER.

Underneath it I've written my own name down, because if I ever find this notebook again I'd like to be certain that it's my handwriting recording these events, that I did what I have done, that it was nobody's fault but mine. And I'll do it again, in braver capitals than my name deserves: <u>JOHN COLE</u>, underlined three times.

I wish I could use some other voice to write this story down. I wish I could take all the books that I've loved best and borrow better words than these, but I've got to make do with an empty notebook and a man who never had a tale to tell and doesn't know how to begin except with the beginning . . .

Last night I slept deeply and too long, and when I woke the sheets were tight as ropes around my legs. My throat felt parched and sore as if I'd been running, and when I put on the gray suit and gray tie I'd laid out the night before, they fit me poorly, like another man's clothes.

Outside, the streets were eerily quiet, and it was the thirtieth day without rain. People had begun to leave town in search of places to hide from the sun, and sometimes I wondered if I'd go out one morning and find I was the last man left. As I hurried to work there were no neighbors to greet me, and all the other shops had lowered their blinds. I'd imagined customers on the steps of the bookshop peering in at the window, wondering what had kept me, knowing I am never late—but of course no one was waiting. No one ever is.

When I let myself in I found that in the dim cool air of the shop I felt sick and faint. There's an armchair I keep beside the till (it was my father's, and whenever I sit there I expect to hear him say, "Be off with you boy!"), and as I reached it my legs buckled and I fell onto the seat. Sweat soaked my shirt and ran into my eyes, and my head hurt, and though I've never understood how anyone could sleep during the day I leaned against the wing of the chair and fell into a doze.

My brother says the shop fits me like a snail's shell, and though I feign indignation to please him he's right— I've never sat in that armchair, or stood behind the till, and not felt fixed in my proper place. But when I woke again just past noon everything had shifted while I slept and nothing was as I'd left it the day before. The clock in the corner sounded ill-tempered and slow, and the carpet was full of unfamiliar birds opening their beaks at me. All the same my headache had receded a little, so I stood and did a few futile little tasks, waiting for someone to come, though I think I knew no one would. I've never much wanted the company of others and I'm sure they don't want mine, but as I fumbled at the books on the shelves I was hoping for the bell above the door to ring, and for someone to stand on the threshold and hear me say, "How can I help you?"

I crossed the empty floor to the window and looked

out on the street. I heard someone calling their dog home and after that it was quieter than ever. For all that I've never believed it possible I felt my heart sink. It was a physical sensation as real as hunger or pain, and just as if it had been pain I felt myself grow chill with sweat. Looking for something to wipe my forehead I put my hand in my pocket, and pulled out a postcard I'd folded and shoved in there a week ago or more.

It showed a boat stranded on a marsh, and a sunrise so bleak and damp you'd think the artist intended to keep visitors away. On it someone had drawn a stick figure walking in the shallows and beckoning me in. I turned it over and saw a question mark written in green crayon, and under it the name CHRISTOPHER in letters an inch high. My brother keeps a room for me in his house on the Norfolk coast, with a narrow bed and a bookshelf where he puts the sort of novels he thinks might interest a man like me. He often says, "Come anytime: anytime, mind you," but I never do, other than at Christmas when it seems the proper thing to do.

I turned the postcard over and over in my hands, and lifted it up as if I could smell salt rising from the marsh. If I went to see my brother, there'd be a house-ful of good-natured boys, and my sister-in-law who seems always to be laughing, and my brother who'd sit up into the small hours talking over whiskey. But I could put up with all of that, I thought, for clean air and a cool wind in the afternoon. So I took a sheet of cardboard from the desk, wrote CLOSED UNTIL FURTHER NOTICE on it in as tidy a set of capitals as I could manage, and propped it in the window. Then I turned off the lights and made my way home.

I'd hoped the weather might be breaking at last, but the sky was blank and bright and my head immediately began to ache. I let myself into my flat and packed a small bag, then left with the haste of a schoolboy playing truant. Twice I walked up and down the road before I found my car, feeling the heat beat like a hammer on the pavement, hardly knowing one end of the street from the other. When at last I saw it, the hood was covered in a fine reddish dust and someone had drawn a five-pointed star on the windshield.

Should I have turned back then? A wiser man might have seen the journey was cursed—on a balcony above me a child was singing (we all fall down!) and in the gutter a pigeon had died on its back—but when I looked up at the windows of the flat they seemed as empty as if no one had lived there for years.

It wasn't until London was an hour behind me that I realized I hadn't brought a map, or even the scrap of paper where once my brother wrote the simplest route to take. I thought I knew the way but my memory's always playing tricks, and in less than two hours I was lost. Black boards by the roadside warned SLOW DOWN and the sun began to scorch my right arm through the glass; I opened the window, but the air that came in was foul with traffic fumes, and I began a convulsive coughing that shook my whole body at the wheel.

I began to panic. My stomach clenched like a fist, and there was a sour taste in my mouth as if I'd already been sick. My heart beat with a kind of fury that repeated itself with a new pain in my head, and I couldn't move my hands on the wheel—nothing about me was doing what it ought and I felt as though I were coming apart in pieces. Then I thought I was losing my sight and when I realized it was nothing but steam coming from under the hood I shouted something—I don't remember what, or why—and gritted my teeth, drifting onto a byroad where the traffic was sparse and slow. When the dark fringes of a familiar forest appeared I was so relieved I could almost have wept.

I drove on a little while, then finding shade pulled over and stood shaking on the bracken verge. The pines stooped over me while I vomited up a few mouthfuls of tea, then I sat on the verge with my head in my hands. When I stood again, feeling ashamed though nobody saw my disgrace, the pain behind my eyes receded and I heard nothing but the engine ticking as it cooled. I was afraid to drive again so soon—I needed to sit a while and rest, and though I know little enough about the workings of my car or any other, I thought the radiator needed water, and that I couldn't be too far from help.

I found I'd driven almost to the road's end, and saw ahead of me a well-trodden path so densely wooded it formed a tunnel of dim green shade. It seemed to suck at me, drawing me deeper in, so that I walked on in a kind of trance. All around I could hear little furtive movements and crickets frantically singing, and there was a lot of white bindweed growing on the verge. After a time—I don't know how long—the path became little more than a dusty track and I found myself at the edge of a dying lawn sloping slightly upward to a distant house.

How can I explain the impression it had on me, to see it high up on the incline, the sun blazing from its windows and pricking the arrow of its weathervane? Everything about it was bright and hard-edged—the slate tiles vivid blue, the chimneys black against the sky, the green door flanked by high white columns from which a flight of steps led down toward the lawn, and to the path where I stood waiting on the boundary.

It seemed to me the most real and solid thing I'd ever seen, and at the same time only a trick of my sight in the heat. As it grew nearer it became less like a dream or invention—there were stains where ivy had been pulled from the walls, and unmatched curtains hanging in the windows. Someone had broken the spine of a book and left it open on the lawn, and near the windows rose-bushes had withered back to stumps. A ginger cat with weeping eyes was stretched out in the shade between them, panting in the sun. The painted door had peeled and blistered in the heat, and as I stood at the foot of the stairs I could see a door knocker shaped like a man's hand raised to rap an iron stone against an iron plate.

I was standing irresolute at the foot of the steps when someone pulled open the door and I heard a child's voice calling. I thought they wanted someone else, who maybe stood behind me and had followed me unnoticed all the way, but when I looked over my shoulder the path was empty and I was all alone. The child laughed and called again, and I heard a name I knew from long ago, though I couldn't think whose face it should call to mind. Then suddenly I realized it was my own name, called over and over, and the shock made me stop suddenly with my foot on the lower step. I thought: it's only the heat, and the ringing in your ears, no one knows you're here.

The child's voice came nearer and nearer, and through the blinding light I made out the figure of a girl, older than I'd first taken her for, running down the steps toward me with her arms outstretched: "John Cole! Is that you? It is you, isn't it—it must be, I'm so glad. I've been waiting for you all day!" I tried to find ways to explain her mistake but in my confusion fumbled with my words, and by then the girl had reached the bottom step and put her arm through mine. She said, "Do you know where to go? Let me show you the way," and drew me up toward the open door. The girl went on talking—about how they'd been looking forward to meeting me, and how late I was, and how glad she was to see me at last—all the while leading me into a stone-flagged hall so dark and cold I began to shiver as the door swung shut behind me.

She must have seen my pallor and my shaking hands, because she began talking to me as if I were an old man, which I suppose I am to her. She said, "It's all right, we're nearly there," as if these were things she'd heard were said to elderly people and thought they'd do all right for me; and all the time I was saying, "Please don't trouble yourself, there's nothing wrong—I'm all right," and neither of us listened to the other.

At the end of the dark hall we went down a stone step dipped in the center and into a large kitchen with a vaulted ceiling. I just had time to register a dozen meat hooks hanging from their chains when she dragged out a stool for me and I nearly fell onto it. The beating behind my eyes stopped like a clock wound down, leaving in its place emptiness and release, as if my head had detached itself and was drifting away. It must have been a little while later that I opened my eyes to see the girl sitting opposite me, her palms resting on the table between us.

She was frowning, and examining me with unworried interest. Then she asked if I wanted water, and without waiting for a reply went over to a stone sink. I saw then how mistaken I'd been—she wasn't a child after all, although she talked like one, rattling on in a light high voice without pausing to breathe or think. She was fairly tall, and her arms and legs were lean but also soft-looking in the way of a child. She was wearing a white T-shirt with a torn pocket on the breast. Her feet were bare and not very clean, and her face was finely made, as though it couldn't possibly have grown out of a muddle of flesh like yours and mine, but must have been carved in stone. When she came back to the table she passed me tepid water in a chipped mug and I saw that her hair was the color of amber, and so were her eyes, and her lips were almost as pale as the skin on her cheeks. It occurred to me that nothing about her was real.

She told me to drink up, although the country water tasted disgusting to me. Perhaps I grimaced, because she said, "I know—let's have tea!" and began to run the tap. The sound of water in the stone sink reminded me of why I'd come, and all over again I started to try and explain. But she wasn't listening—I might as well have been an animal she'd found on the steps. She said, "I've got to look after you, you see. They said: 'make sure he's got everything he needs,' and I said: 'I can do it, you know, I'm not stupid.'" I still felt light-headed and could hear bells ringing in my ears, and comforted myself with the idea that the girl, the stone sink, the kettle in her hands, were not real, nor anything at all to do with me. The cat I'd seen outside appeared suddenly on the table in front of me, moving its tail like a hypnotist's watch, and I sat following its swing. The table was scored with knife cuts and scorched with hot pans, and someone had scratched into the wood the words NOT THIS TIME.

The girl said, "Everything's ready for you—all your things are there. I got your room ready myself. They told me off because I picked the last flowers left in the garden but I think you'll like them and besides, tomorrow they'll all be dead."

She picked up a box of matches to light the stove, striking too hard so the first few broke and fell with the smell of sulphur. The cat looked at me, then flattened its ragged ears and bolted. I ought really to have been afraid of the strangeness and the dark and the insistent child, and those appalling meat hooks hanging from their chains, but instead it all seemed so absurd, and so like something in a novel, that I began to laugh. I tried to swallow the laughter but it stuck in my throat and came bursting up again, so that when the girl turned to face me she must have thought I was crying, because she ran over and patting my shoulder said, "Oh dear, oh dear, there's no need for that," which only made me laugh harder. Then she said fretfully, "And I promised them I'd look after you, didn't I?" and started wringing her hands.

The laughter made the pain in my head so fierce that the kitchen and the girl's face were obscured by bright specks of light. I stopped suddenly and put my hand over my eyes and said carefully, "It's just that my head hurts, you see, and my heart isn't beating right—" I clapped a hand to my chest as if I'd be able to force it back into its proper rhythm and said much too loudly, "After all I only wanted water for the car . . ." When I tried to stand, the ringing in my ears grew more persistent but also farther away, as if it came from another room. The girl ran to my side and thrust herself under my arm and said, "I think I'd better take you upstairs, don't you?" I remember looking down at the top of her head and seeing her amber hair ringed with brightness where the lights in the ceiling struck it. It was so like a painted halo that it set me off laughing again, stopping me from speaking and saying she was mistaken, and that someone else must be on their way, perhaps was there already on the doorstep, waiting for her to come and fetch them in.

Instead I let her lead me up a flight of stairs to a long corridor carpeted with thinning rugs, and it seemed to me that we passed a dozen doors before she paused at one and kicked it open, saying, "Here we are now, there you are—you can have a sleep." She pushed me into the room and closed the door behind me as if she were glad to have finally finished the task she'd been given, and I heard her running away down the hall.

I stood swaying on the threshold and saw in front of me a narrow bed with a peeling white iron frame and a patchwork bedspread, an empty bookshelf, and a pair of windows that tapered to a point. In a corner of the room a narrow door stood half-open, and I could see through it a bathroom tiled in blue. From a plain oak frame propped in the corner a painted Puritan with a square white collar eyed me over his Bible, and beside him there was a wooden desk and chair. In a jug on a stool beside the bed a few flowers had used up their water and slumped on their stems, and as I watched one fell rustling to the floor. At the foot of the bed was a heap of boxes sealed with brown tape. There was a large white label on each lid, and the labels all bore the same name, and the name was mine.

I don't know what I did then—I only remember seeing my name over and over, and putting my thumbs to the pain in my eye sockets to try and push it away—but I must have collapsed onto the narrow bed and fallen at once into a deep sleep.

Much later I was woken by more of that insistent ringing in my ears, but as I listened it became more and more distant until I realized it was coming from downstairs. It was like the ringing of a bell, tolling the same note, growing louder then fading until I couldn't hear it anymore. Then the single note became a peal and eventually a melody I half remembered, and I knew it wasn't a bell after all but a piano, expertly and patiently played. I stood, feeling the blood drain from my head and into my fingertips, then went to the windows to see where I was. Immediately below me I saw a stone terrace, bordered by more of those dying roses, although someone must have been watering these and a few parchment-colored flowers clung on. Around the edge of the terrace was a stone balustrade with pieces missing, so that the barrier to the lawn was broken. In the middle of the terrace I could see a sundial on a stone column, but when I leaned closer to try and see how long I'd slept I saw its blade was crooked and told two times at once.

This room overlooks land at the back of the house, and I couldn't see the forest or the path I'd taken. Below me there's a greenhouse and a terrace, then the dry lawn slopes downward for a hundred yards or so, and becomes a stretch of scrub where brambles and nettles have taken over. Beyond there (and I've never seen anything like it before) I could see a steep embankment rising to perhaps fifteen feet. Though all around it the lawn is parched and dry, the grass on the embankment is vivid green, as though it's found a source of water it's too selfish to share. You could scramble up it, if you tried, although I don't know what could be on the other side. On the right, almost out of view, I could make out a folly of a building: a little redbrick tower with an arched wooden door, and a yellow light high up on a crenellated roof. It's this light that reaches me here, as bright as if someone's behind me shining a torch on the page. It looks so out of place I half expect to see a pair of knights-at-arms come tumbling out, with the yellow light shining from the blades of their lances.

While I stood at the window, wondering how far I'd strayed from my path and how long I'd have to walk before I found my car, someone knocked on the door. I jumped like a guilty child, then the knock came again, and the girl who'd brought me upstairs put her head slowly into the room. She'd put up her hair, and the effect of that lovely face seeming to float in the dark space behind the door was so strange it stopped me from speaking. She smiled at me and said, "Oh good, I'm glad you're awake. Dinner's ready. Are you better now? You look better. Come down, I've saved you a seat and everyone's waiting."

It's thirty years since I conquered my stammer, but it came back then, taking hold of my tongue so that none of the words I had ready (something like: You've been so kind, but really I think there's been a mistake . . .) came out. While I stood stupidly mouthing at the air the girl in the doorway flung up her hand and reared away, because downstairs someone was calling her. She rolled her eyes at me and said, "I'd better go. I'll see you down there—you know where to find us." Then she slammed the door and I was left alone again.

I can't remember the last time I felt anger: I can't help thinking it's a weakness I despise and pity. But the confusion and aimlessness that had dogged me all day vanished, and were replaced by a pure burst of fury. Here at last was a moment of perfect clarity: I must be the butt of an unkind joke. I imagined conspirators laughing in a room downstairs, my brother pouring them all wine; but recalling the boxes, with my name on each, the anger gave way to unease. My memory had never been trustworthy—was there some other plan I'd forgotten—did they know me, after all? I knelt at the foot of the bed and drew toward me a large leather bag, and the painted Puritan, spotting a sin, raised an eyebrow as I undid the straps.

What did I expect to see—my own clothes pressed and folded, the books I'd lately been reading? My pulse leaped and I flinched as if something might have been waiting to take my hand—but there was nothing inside but clothes that smelled of another man's sweat, and a few objects wrapped in plastic bags. A white label hung from the leather handle and I lifted it to the light and saw that it wasn't my name written there as I had thought, but something as different as it was the same: JON COULES, in the thick ink of a felt-tipped pen. It was repeated over all the other boxes tumbled at the end of the bed, and at the sight of it the world settled around me: I felt as though I might be coming off a long sea trip to stand on solid ground. I wasn't supposed to be here, of course I wasn't—no one wanted me and there was no reason I should stay.

So I smoothed my hair, undid my tie and knotted it again, and went downstairs. The notes from the piano had stopped, and I could hear voices muddling in the easy way of people who've spoken so often they don't need manners anymore. There was the sound of cutlery thrown down, plates passed from hand to hand and bottles knocking against glass rims. Now and then someone laughed with a sound that wasn't quite sincere, the sort that's meant to please the teller of a tale, and I followed the laughter toward the darker end of the hall where a door stood open a little, and through which spilled out light and the scent of cooked meat. I could smell along with the meat my own sweat, and I knew I looked disheveled and foolish. But I thought I'd despise myself if I turned like a coward and left without saying good-bye to the girl or explaining her kind mistake. So I drew in a breath that did nothing to settle my stomach, and pushed open the door.

Seated at a long table five people went on talking and eating as though they hadn't seen me come in. The table reflected the blue-gray paper on the walls, and the dim lights in the ceiling and the lamps on the sideboard were shaded in blue glass—it looked like they were dining underwater. Behind the table a pair of glass doors blurred with the heat of their bodies overlooked the terrace I'd seen from my window, and I could make out the sundial's slanted blade shining in the yellow light at the garden's end. A big moth beat its wings against a lamp and set soft shadows moving on the walls, and a painting with colors darkened and cracked in pieces showed a bearded man with a clever shy face. He was sitting at a table holding a steel ruler and a pair of compasses so large they might have been a weapon, and another moth had settled on his painted hand. At the head of the table a man rather older than me sat in an oak chair like a bishop's throne. A branched candlestick stuck up from the high back of the chair, and someone had only just blown out the candles, so that his head was wreathed in bluish smoke. He didn't seem to notice, but sat staring at his plate and drumming his fingers on the table. He too had a long beard and was so like the painting on the wall that I kept looking from one to the other and wouldn't have been surprised to see either of them turn to me and speak.

The chairs on either side of him were empty, and to his left the girl who'd welcomed me in sat spreading butter thickly on a roll. The roll was hot, and melted butter ran into the crook of her elbow. She didn't notice, or didn't care, but went on chatting in an amiable inconsequential way I recognized as fondly as if I already knew her well. Another woman sat at the foot of the table with her back to me. She had thick gray hair fastened at the crown with a broken pencil. On the right of the man in the bishop's chair, a tall boy with black curly hair so glossy it picked up the blue light of the lamps sat turned away from me. I remember thinking how fragile and white his neck looked, with the bone at the top of his spine casting a blue shadow. He was listening attentively to a gray-haired man who leaned back in his chair with an indolence I immediately disliked. The man wore a white shirt unbuttoned at the neck, and he was inspecting the nails on his left hand and murmuring quietly. The table was covered with far more food than they could possibly have needed, on chipped platters showing blurred flowers like old stains, and there were several open bottles of wine.

With my hand on the door I waited for someone to see me standing there, and the wait went on and on until I couldn't bear it anymore and shoved the door so that it knocked against an empty chair. Immediately they all fell silent: a knife was dropped and hastily snatched up and the moth paused midflight and turned to look at me. Then the girl with the amber hair stood and said, "Look, it's John! Look everyone, he's here!" She dashed round the table, took my hand, and pulled me farther into the room. And I couldn't resist, of course—she smiled up at me as if she'd been waiting all day to have me there, as though I were something she wanted to show off. "I told you I'd look after him, didn't I," she said. "Well, I did, and here he is."

I think I said "Hello," or "Good evening," but before I could pull my arm away and begin to explain, the older woman stood and turned to face me. She was very tall, so that her eyes were almost level with mine, and she came toward me with her arms outstretched. I found my hands going up to meet hers, not from any impulse of my own but as if she compelled them to her. She held on to me and said, in what was both a welcome and a chastisement: "Finally. You look pale—have you slept? Well—I'm Hester, of course."

I said, "Of course," because it was expected and because she startled me. Her eyes were black and fiercely lit: I couldn't tell where the iris ended and the pupil began. It was like being put under a magnifying glass and inspected for flaws or virtues, and it made me flush more than ever and think how unfit those clear fine eyes were to the rest of her. I never think much about appearance, my own or anyone else's, and I don't think I'd ever thought of someone as ugly before. But for her it's the only word that will do: everything about her seemed poorly assembled, as though she'd been put together from leftover pieces—her eyes set under a deeply lined forehead, her nose crooked like a child's drawing of a witch, her skin thick and coarse. It looked to me as if she must have stolen her wonderful eyes from someone else. I didn't notice her body then, but remember it now, her heaviness as she sat passing wine or getting up to look out of the glass doors—she was padded everywhere with flesh so there was no distinction between her shoulders and her waist, and had covered herself in a shabby dark blue dress. Her ankles were swollen in the heat and she wore ugly leather sandals with broken straps.

I went on saying, "Of course, of course," letting her hold my hands, while she looked at me as though she knew what I was thinking and wasn't hurt, but found it amusing. Then she pushed me toward a chair, and gesturing around the table said, "Clare you know of course. This is Elijah"—the man in the high-backed chair nodded gravely and went on tapping at the table—"Have you met Walker? No? Walker, pour our guest a glass of wine. White, I think, John?" I nodded. The gray-haired man leaned forward rather slowly, and passed me a glass that was much too full. He gave me a disinterested look, shrugged faintly, and turned back to the boy beside him. Hester flung out her hand toward the boy and said, "Eve, my darling, remember your manners." Then she leaned and whispered to me, "I do what I can with them all, but really . . ." I took a sip of wine and the black-haired boy turned reluctantly from the man beside him to look at me. I spilled my wine, which was so cold on my shirt I shivered—it wasn't a boy at all, but a young woman who must have cut her own hair in a fit of rage or boredom, because it stood out from her head in irregular curls, some of them clinging to the sheen of sweat on her forehead.

She stood and reached across the table to shake my hand. Hers was as small as a child's and her nails were dirty. She was very slender, and I could see how fine and sharp her bones were, with a thin covering of white skin glossy in the heat. In a voice on the verge of singing she said: "You must be hungry, John. Do sit, won't you? And don't let Walker frighten you: he will, you know— if he can." She gestured toward the man sitting next to her, who concealed a smile, then struck a match on the table's edge and lit a cigarette.

I think I said that yes, I was hungry; then straightened my shoulders, raised my voice, and prepared to explain their mistake. But from all sides hands appeared, passing me a plate piled with roast lamb and sliced tomatoes, and more wine, and torn pieces of bread that burned my fingers, and the old stammer kept me quiet. Clare, the girl who'd brought me in, kept smiling as if I were a particular friend of hers that no one had believed would come, and I couldn't think how to get out of it without making her look foolish. I felt as if I'd tried to cross a small stream, sure I'd reach the bank in a stride or two, and suddenly found myself in a strong current, borne out to sea.

Sometimes they spoke to me, saying, "Isn't it better now, without the sun, and wouldn't you be glad if it never rose again?" or "The salt, John, would you mind?" and then seemed to forget I was there. I remember it all in fragments: the black-haired young woman taking her companion's cigarette and drawing so deeply her eyes ran, but refusing to cough; amber-haired Clare leaning her head on Hester's shoulder and instantly sleeping; the tap-tap-tap of the older man's fingers on the chair. Then I began to notice a sort of watchfulness, as though they were waiting for something to happen. Now and then the older woman looked up to the glass doors and then down at her plate with a frown. Once she saw me catch her out in an anxious glance and I believe she looked for a fraction of a second guilty, before passing me meat that had grown cold.

A little later, as I was beginning to think with relief that I was dreaming, somebody else came in. He was young, no more than twenty-five, and I guessed from the color of his hair and eyes that he was Clare's brother. His clothes were wet, and he'd grazed the knuckles of his left hand. He looked weary but jubilant and said, "You know, I think it might be all right, after all . . . Maybe I've been wrong all this time and everything's safe and sound . . ." He stooped over his sister, his bright head touching hers, took her plate and began to finish off her meal, talking between mouthfuls about a water

level somewhere and house martins making their nests.
Then the girl whispered into his ear, and gulping down a
piece of bread he wiped his hand on his shirt and thrust
it toward me. "Oh—didn't see you there—turned up
all right, then? I hope it's not too much for you, shut up
in here with us all . . ." He gestured around the table
and they all laughed, affectionately but also too loudly,
as though they were indulging a child who'd spoken
out of turn. I said that no, of course it wasn't too much,
and wondered why it was they all seemed to be straining toward him across the table, sometimes reaching out
to touch him on the shoulder, or brush dust from his
sleeve. Once the older woman came to crouch by his
side, steadying herself on the table's edge and saying:
"What were you up to last night? I heard banging downstairs as though you were breaking up the furniture—
I almost called the police!" He looked up, baffled, as
though she must have been talking to someone else, but
she shrugged and squeezed his shoulder and said, "Ah
well—no harm done." For a few moments he was silent
and troubled; then he shook his head violently as though
to clear it and asked, smiling, if there was more to eat.

So it went on, I don't know for how much longer,
and when the wine was gone they drifted out into the
garden. Only the older man stayed, sometimes turning
with an anxious look toward the glass doors to the ter-

race where the young man stood with his arm around his sister's shoulders.

I ought to have roused myself then, and found courage or reason or whatever it was I'd been missing all day. But the drink made me slow and foolish, and I might have stayed all night at the threshold watching and listening, if a phone had not begun to ring just on the other side of the door. Elijah seemed not to hear it, nor the others in the garden; it went on and on, the shrill alarm of one of those old-fashioned phones that were only ever used for bad news.

The sound of it brought on my headache again, and broke through the indolence that had settled on me with the heat and the wine. I got up and followed the sound to a low table at the foot of the stairs and stood looking down at the receiver waiting for someone to come running. Then it stopped, and the silence was so complete I heard the cat purring in another room. I sat on the bottom step and looked at the front door. The key was in the lock and on the other side was the road home, and there was no one to see me leave. I began pulling myself to my feet—I knew I'd been foolish to stay as long as I had, and little better than a liar and a thief when you thought about it, taking their food and their kindness—then I realized that of course I was drunk—my head ached, my legs were slow and heavy.

I could no more drive home than run there. I sat heavily against the stairs, jarring my spine against the step. Then the phone began to ring again, and with a sort of reflex action that had nothing to do with me I snatched it up and said, "Hello?" At the other end someone was shouting. It was a bad line, from a cell phone or a phone booth, and I could hear traffic and noisy passersby. A man's voice said, "Hello? Hello? Is anybody there? Hester, is that you?"

"No," I said. "No, she isn't here." And then, because for my own sake I wanted to hear my name spoken I said, "It's John Cole."

But the other man couldn't hear me, or wasn't listening, only went on shouting against the passing cars: "Hello? Is anybody there? Hester—is that you?"

"No," I said. "I'm afraid she isn't here." My voice when I heard it was brisk and impatient, as I imagine a secretary's might be. Then he swore and said, "Well, take a message, can't you?" I said that I would, of course, and he said: "Tell her it's Jon Coules here, Jonathan Coules, and I'm delayed—I'll be a week at least—" The line broke, and when it returned it was clear he'd given some explanation I only caught at the end: "—couldn't be helped . . . have you got that—have you got it? A week, and I'll be with you."

While I write this I imagine I have a reader, one who

doesn't know me, who doesn't believe a word I've written here, or—and would this be worse?—believes me, but finds me too dull, my handwriting too cramped, to read any further. Well—if you're there, holding this page nearer to the light to see more clearly, wishing I'd told you more, hoping I might do better on the next page, or the next—I want to make you understand that what I did next wasn't a plan. I didn't do it out of malice or mischief. Do you believe me? Can you believe it could have been an impulse that was nothing to do with me, that I didn't know was coming, or I would have done everything I could do to prevent it?

When I looked up from where I sat, Hester was standing in front of me. Her dark blue dress was black and damp under the arms and in an irregular patch at the base of her throat; her hair had come loose in greasy coils that seemed to have an animation all of their own; and her broad ugly face was oily with sweat. But in the dark hall her dark eyes glowed, and she stooped and put her hand on the crown of my head where the hair is thin, and her palm felt hot and gentle against my skin. Then she said, "You must be tired." She said it so kindly, and so certainly, that I realized at once how many years it had been since anyone had noticed whether I was tired or not. Then she said, "Go up now, go on. Go up before the others come in. Sleep as long as you can. Nothing will happen here tonight or tomorrow, nothing ever does." Then she glanced down at the telephone and said, "Did I hear that earlier? Did you answer it, my dear? How rude of me—you didn't come here to be my secretary, after all!" She laughed, and so did I. Then she said, "Was there any message?" and began wearily pinning back her hair.

How many times have I read of those moments when minutes accommodate years, and lives are recalled in the pouring of a drink? I've never believed a word of it, but in the space it took me to draw a breath the day replayed itself: I saw the branches of the pines closing over my head, the narrow path and the dying lawn, the face of the girl with the amber hair, wonderfully made and stooping over me as I sat at the table. And all the while I remembered also the last I'd seen of my flat, with its empty windows on the empty street, and the shop's clock ticking slower than any other clock I've known.

Then I heard myself say, as if it was someone else's voice in another room: "Oh, nothing, it was nothing—there was nobody there."

II

"Nothing," John said, and had the grace to meet the woman's eye—though, certain she'd see a little of his lie, he'd quickly turned away and leaned his head against the wall. *Nothing will come of nothing*, he thought, and didn't believe a word of it. Hester took his sigh for weariness, and smiling said: "Then go up, and sleep without dreaming." She seemed almost to thrust him ahead of her up the stairs, though she remained there at the foot of them watching him go until he turned the corner and must have gone from view. He'd lingered a while in the corridor—someone called up, *Oh, John don't forget to say your prayers*, and laughing went away—then fumbled at the nearest door. The first was locked; the second shrieked on its hinges; the third, already open, showed a room so heaped with clothes the furniture was lost. When he came to the fourth it seemed already familiar, with a particular mark on the wood; pushing it open, he saw again the narrow bed and the child's desk where now—with a gesture of shame and distaste—he pushed the notebook away.

A kind of painful clarity came over him: dishonest to blame confusion or drink, or claim it was a kindness to the girl who'd welcomed him in; making an account of his own deceit made it necessary to admit that no one had forced his hand. Appalled, he said: "What have I done—what have I *done*?" and might have returned to the notebook and made a kind of confession if he had not heard a violent knocking on the door.

The sound tugged him from his seat; he knocked over the lamp in his haste and the bulb broke against the bare boards. Flushing violently, feeling again the weight of Hester's kindness, he thought: *They must have known all along—we have all been lying!* He patted at his disordered clothes, preparing to meet what must surely be a furious delegation, fumbling for a means to excuse himself. But the knocking subsided to a patient tap, and the door opened, too slowly for anger, to reveal the young man who'd joined their table late. He'd combed his auburn hair into a side parting and put on a gray T-shirt on which was printed a large and unblinking pair of eyes.

"Game of cards, John, unless it's an early night you're after? Come and join us: Walker's been trying to corrupt Elijah all week—drinking last week, gambling this—and we could use another player."

And so he was helpless again, as the boy took his arm, just as if he'd done so a dozen times or more, while on his chest the blind eyes closed and opened. Speechless with reprieve John let himself be led down the ill-lit hall, and said, "Trouble is I haven't played poker since college. Always folded early—I'm a terrible liar, you see."

"It won't matter, you won't be any worse than Elijah—you haven't spoken to him yet, have you? You haven't spoken to him *here*, I mean . . ." Alex paused, and his arm in John's tightened and withdrew. He seemed uncertain whether he'd spoken too soon, or too much, and looked quickly at John as though testing the air. Then seeming satisfied he said, "Well—he's a good man. A bit odd"—he tapped his forehead, in a kind of self-mocking gesture—"but I like him—always did, you know, even then."

The dim hall led away from the head of the stairs, the floorboards pockmarked and pale with dust by the baseboards. John could smell cigarette smoke, and behind that the sweet scent of damp and dust that only ever signals a roomful of books.

The thin cat woke from its dark corner and tried to trip John, who gave it a furtive kick, and said: "No, we've never spoken—though I watched him tonight, standing there at the window and not coming out, as though he's afraid of the dark—what is it? What bothers him?"

Alex, pausing at the threshold, said: "If you ask him he'll say, 'It's trouble with my heart.' And if you ask him what trouble, he'll say, 'It's heavy.' There's not much wrong with him really," he went on, turning the door handle. Then, as if he'd heard what John had barely thought, he grinned and with a careless affectionate blow to the shoulder said, "At least, not much more than the rest of us. Now then"—the door swung open, and revealed Elijah sitting with Walker at a bare plywood table—"Hit me!"

"Too late for all that." Walker, his shirt unbuttoned a little too far, deftly shuffled a pack of cards and knocked them on his knee. "Turns out the Preacher's not a natural gambler. That old face is too truthful—we might as well be using glass cards. How much did you lose?"

"One hundred and seventy-three pence." The older man tugged, regretful, at his beard. "You didn't tell me it was all about lying. I'm no good at that."

"So I see. Sit down, won't you?" said Walker to John. "You're always so keen on standing about."

John, obedient, sat at the table. It was stained and burned in places, and scattered with piles of copper coins and a discarded deck of cards too dog-eared for use. On one of the playing cards someone had printed *EADWACER* in cramped capitals, and John drew them toward him and began a slow careful shuffle. Beside him Elijah tapped out a slow beat on the table, and accompanied it with a low humming that seemed to resonate and shiver in the wood. The melody had an insistent familiar lilt, and John could almost have ended its phrases himself.

A tin of Drum tobacco and several torn cigarette papers lay on the table, and there were two empty teacups that smelled strongly of whiskey. Aside from the table, the room was the same as his own: there again was the narrow bed with its painted metal frame, and the same shabby shelves, though John saw enviously that these bowed under the weight of cloth- and leather-bound books.

Behind him the uncurtained windows overlooked the lawn and showed a sickle moon. "Close the door," said Alex, "or Hester will hear, and I've had enough of her today." He rolled his eyes affectionately, and Walker reached out with his foot to shut the door. Its swing set up a faint rustle from somewhere behind John; wondering what caused it, he turned to see that where the walls were bare of shelves they were covered, from roof to floor, in sheets of thin white paper printed with columns of black type. Each sheet was pinned at the upper corners and left free at its lower edge, so that they lifted in the wake of the door. John would have liked to reach forward and tug one from the wall to read it, but felt Walker's pale eyes on him and affected not to have noticed.

"What do you think?" said Elijah, pointing over John's shoulder. "It's my patented storm prediction system."

"I see," said John, who saw nothing. "And does it work?"

"Well, I don't know yet, do I? But it's a simple matter of wind direction." He surveyed the wall, clasping his hands across his stomach and tipping his head to one side. "Or, indeed, of there being any wind at all . . . Listen." He stood, then flapped his hands at the wall as if shooing it away. The paper shuffled noisily then settled in its regiments. "Imagine how loudly that'll sound when the storm comes! I don't want to miss it if I'm asleep." Alex caught his eye, and again made that faint tapping gesture on his forehead. Stifling a smile, John bent to read the nearest sheets of paper, and at once recognized them as pages torn from a Bible large enough to have rested on a pulpit lectern. Some had been cut neatly with a razor, and others were carelessly torn, bringing with them fragments of the white thread that had stitched them to the spine. On every sheet the phrase *be not afraid* appeared, the verse circled in uneven loops of red ink.

"Are you a drinker?" said Walker. He withdrew a bottle of whiskey from underneath the table, and pulled out the stopper. In the close air of the room, the smell of peat and alcohol stung John's eyes.

"Not much of one," he said apologetically, turning back from the table. "I don't mind the taste but it makes me dream when I'd rather not."

Walker's eyes glinted gunmetal gray. "Don't drink," he said. "Don't smoke. What do you do?" John blushed; he was conscious of having made an opening that could be probed wider if anyone cared to try. He opened the Drum tin, and picked at the shreds of tobacco on the table. "Alex tells me you're being corrupted," he said to Elijah, polite as a remark on the weather. The older man nodded gravely and began again the distracted humming; then he sighed, and said: "Walker's doing his best, and of course I'm grateful for his efforts; but I'm not taking to it as easily as I feared."

"We've done drink," said Walker, picking up a box of matches and sliding the drawer in and out of its case, "but not with much success. He's far too big a man—

look at him: size of an ox. Smoking makes him feel sick—he turns green before the match goes out. Gambling's a waste of time; it's like playing with a child. I'm running out of vices, although there's always women and song . . ." Alex set a penny spinning on its edge; the fabric of his T-shirt moved in folds and the painted eyes shifted anxiously to the door.

"And do you mind my asking," said John, feeling his way through the conversation with outstretched hands, "why you're doing all this?" The penny rattled to a halt.

"He had a wasted youth," said Walker, striking a match and idly watching the flame flare down to his fingertips.

John looked at Elijah's grave unsmiling face, and his forearms solid as oak, and could not imagine him either a youth or a wastrel.

"Wasted it on God," said Alex, with his habit of answering unasked questions. He rolled the coin across the table with his thumb. "On God, and on doing good." At a loss, John decided he'd wait patiently for someone to say something sensible, and began neatly stacking coins. Elijah, taking pity, leaned back in his chair, folded his hands across his dark-shirted stomach, and said gently: "You ought not to mock our visitor." His voice, though rather quieter than that of the other men, was deep and grave, as though it came to them from a pulpit. Walker and Alex both looked a little ashamed of themselves, and Elijah, content with his reproof, turned to John. "I wasn't always like this, you know. I was a pastor, I was respected . . ." He thought about this, and then said, as if it had just occurred to him: "Admired, actually, and I believe I was loved—but lives change, even at my age— suddenly—quite without warning . . ." He paused again, and John thought he saw the man's heavily lidded eyes brighten with moisture. "How can I explain? It was as if I were coming home after a long day, tired and hungry and with aching feet. And there at the end of the road was my house and all the lights were on. And there was the front door I painted and beside it the bay tree I planted the day my daughter was born. But when I tried my keys they wouldn't turn in the lock, and there were faces at the window but they were strangers and they all turned away . . ."

Elijah drew the whiskey toward him and surveyed the label. It showed a watercolor picture of a distillery set on an outcrop of reddish rock. The rainstorm gathering above the rocks looked to John like an impossible miracle he'd never see again. "I think I'll have another, if you don't mind," said Elijah. When Walker had passed him a half-filled teacup, he went on, "No, I'm telling it wrong—it wasn't like that at all. Look—if I drop this cup, what will happen?"

"It will fall and break," said John, glad for once to be certain of things.

"Of course. You know that to be true, because you've dropped things many times before. Things fall and break—those are the rules. But what if I let go and it simply hung there, or fell slowly, or began to rise up? Would you believe it? Not the first time, you wouldn't— you know the rules, after all. You wouldn't believe your eyes—you'd think yourself mad, or unwell—you'd do it again and again, until you really believed the rules had changed. And then you'd think: what else has changed? If that rule can be broken, what about all the others? And maybe you'd want to put your hand in a fire, and see if it came out wet." He drained the cup. "It was like that. All my life I'd lived by a set of rules as fixed and constant as the sun setting in the west. They made sense of everything in the past, and nothing in the future frightened me. It was a rock under my feet. I'm talking about God," he said anxiously, leaning forward a little, as though he wanted to be very certain John understood. "You realize that?"

"I think so, yes."

"Good." He reached for the bottle, thought better of it, and instead ran a finger around the lip of the teacup, and sucked thoughtfully at it. "You see, I believed—no, I *knew*—that my life had been ordered since before time. I knew that events would follow each other in their proper order, and always for my good. There'd be storms of course, but sunshine not long after. Illness, but then good health. Disappointments—more of those than I like to remember—but always cause for hope. And I never once thought, This simply is the way of life. I thanked God that he was the overseer—that he was holding up the sky, if you like. And I became a pastor, because nothing mattered more to me than making others see that they too were in the hands of God. And then one morning"—John thought for a moment the older man was going to make the teacup disappear up his sleeve—"he was gone. Just like that. I woke up and he wasn't there . . . or was it like that? I must try to be truthful . . ." He rolled the cup between his palms and John flinched, certain it would break. "Maybe it happened more slowly, like waking alone in your bed with no head on the pillow next to yours, and mourning a while before realizing you've always been alone, and the footsteps you'd heard out in the hall were only echoes of your own. I expect it happens every day—children grow up and grow out of their faith, or life makes the case against God. But in my case, of course, everyone noticed, because they all went to church one Sunday morning and there was no one in the pulpit."

Walker coughed discreetly, and lit a cigarette. In the

unmoving air the ribbon of smoke lifted to the ceiling where it spread and thinned. "They waited almost a quarter of an hour, didn't they? Sang the same hymn three times."

"They did," said Elijah, and began to tap the table again, this time accompanying the beat with a deep, half-heard hum. John thought he knew the melody, and then, in a sudden moment of perfect clarity, remembered where he'd heard it before. His had not been a pious upbringing, but his mother had been a dutiful churchgoer and she alone could coax the church's piano into life. Her favorite hymn had a mournful lilting melody (found on a seashore by a Welsh vicar, she said, written on a scrap of paper and rolled into a bottle). The melancholy words would move the congregation to tears, and John remembered them now: how the love of God was *vast, unmeasured, boundless, free, rolling like a mighty ocean in its fullness over me* . . . As a boy he'd imagined gray folds of saltwater closing over his head, and not fighting upward for air and life but sinking instead with his hands folded in prayer. Twenty-five years later—his mother and the music she'd played too distant and vague to remember—he felt the old unease return.

The older man was staring abstractedly at the paper-covered walls, preoccupied with the old song. "It's all gone, you see—all gone. The rock under my feet turned out to be sand after all, and in the end the tide came in. Walker says I'm free, like a dog off its leash. Which is all very well, but what if I run into the road?"

"We'll show you where to cross," said Walker, smilingly. He looked at Elijah with more warmth and affection than John would have thought him capable of summoning, and began deftly shuffling the pack of cards. "Shall we try again, Preacher?" he said. "Practice makes perfect, even with sin." He dealt them each a hand of three. Sitting with the other men around the table, the whiskey bottle between them and the moon passing the open window, was curiously like being onboard a half-empty ship, forced to find company in a stranger's cabin. It reminded John of a pamphlet he'd once bought at auction, a coarse engraving of a ship under full sail printed on the cover. "I'll tell you something interest- ing," he said rather eagerly, leaning forward. "Last year, or the year before, I bought a crateful of books that had been left to get damp in a garage somewhere. Most of them were ruined—one of the books even had a kind of fat blind maggot burrowed in its spine—but there were a few things worth having, and the best of them was a facsimile of a German poem—from the fifteenth century, I think, though I can't remember who wrote it—called 'The Ship of Fools,' about a boat put to sea full of madmen. No sane man or woman was allowed aboard, except the captain, I suppose, though surely he was mad to take such a crew? At sea of course they'd do as they please—there's no law, and no one watching; and if no one's watching, who's to say what's sane, and what isn't? I didn't read all of it, but I liked the idea, and ever since I've wondered if it ever really happened. Madmen turned out of towns and villages and sent to sea, and allowed to get on with being mad as hatters, without bothering anyone by it."

He paused, aware the other men were avoiding his eyes. Walker put out his cigarette half-smoked and shuffled intently through his hand of cards, and Alex began to gnaw at the scab between his knuckles. John felt something in the room shift and fracture; he said, "I expect I've gotten it wrong. I often do."

Beside him Alex set coins spinning on the table until a dozen of them reeled between the tobacco tin and the bottle of whiskey, buzzing as they went. Walker laid down his cards in a tidy arc, then stood up and lightly touched Alex on the shoulder with a tentative gesture. "I'm off," he said. "It's late—are you coming?" The younger man stared miserably at the buzzing coins, which all at once ceased spinning and clattered to a halt. The painted eyes on his shirt blinked with undisguised malice, and he gave John a hostile and secretive look, as if he suspected him of having been spying for a weakness all along. It was so unlike the affectionate lad who'd threaded an arm through his and drawn him into their game that he flinched as if it had been a blow. Walker stood aside to let the boy pass into the dark hall, then with an ironic bow vaguely in John's direction closed the door behind him.

Elijah sighed, reaching across to push the window open a little farther, so that the scent of dry grass seeped over the windowsill.

He surveyed John for a while without speaking, then reached for the bottle. "I think perhaps we should talk," he said. John took the cup he was offered, recoiling as the whiskey fumes stung his eyes: *So I haven't gotten away with it after all*, he thought, with greater relief than regret. Elijah wiped a droplet from his mustache, and gazed without speaking at the other man over steepled fingers. His eyes, above the russet square-cut beard, were mild and frank, reacting readily to the glow and fade of light. As he turned them now on John the pupils spread and darkened his gaze; he said, with a suggestion of mischief, "But not, I think, tonight: there are some things best kept for morning, and a kinder light—can you remember the way to your room?"

Thursday

I

John was woken by ringing that came not from the piano he'd heard the night before, but from a newly hollow place inside his skull. Through the pink net of veins in his lowered lids he saw the sun filling the room to its corners, and began to raise himself on his elbows. Pain surged from the back of his neck to his forehead then receded in a sickening wave. He sat cross-legged on the sheets, carefully counting air in and out of his lungs and swallowing bile. His bladder was painfully full, and when he was sure he could stand without vomiting he crossed the room to the small bathroom. He sat to relieve himself, wondering how long it would be before he was sick, and whether afterward he'd be himself again. The little room was surprisingly cool: he shivered, and saw gooseflesh break out on his knees, but in time the chill settled his stomach, and he sat there a long while fixing his eyes on the sink, willing the world to shrink to the proportions of the blue bar of soap in its cracked clay dish.

A little while later, with nausea stirring his stomach, he stood half-dressed at the window. It was another day without any sign of rain, another morning without birdsong; in the clear early light the garden below looked diminished and ordinary, the folly at the end a prop for an abandoned play and the greenhouse stained and shabby. The windows were thickly glazed in uneven panes that threw back a mottled reflection nothing like the neat-edged image in his own mirror every morning. The face he saw now was too pale and lean, the hair too long, and under heavy lids glossed with sweat the pale eyes glittered. He raised his right hand, uncertain whether the other man would raise his left in the proper greeting. "What came over you?" he said. "What in God's name have you done?" The watching man had no reply, and John returned to the edge of the bed, cradling his aching head in his hands: what *had* he done, after all? Nothing brave or impassioned, not the brief lapse into madness to be expected of a man arriving suddenly in middle age, but an abuse of kindness and trust: he'd been welcomed and cared for—he touched the place where the woman had put a kind hand—and in return he'd deceived them all. Recalling the words of the preacher the night before (*I think perhaps we should talk*) he felt the unease of a child awaiting the headmaster's summons.

In the sober light of morning, away from the gaze of a dozen eyes, there'd be no difficulty in slipping downstairs and making his way through the forest to his car (he imagined it sinking already into the dense verge, its windows curtained with an overnight fall of pine needles), back on the road to his brother, or to his ordinary ordered life. He thought it must be early still, though outside on the terrace the sundial was lying. He pressed an ear to the door, but the house was silent: his heart quickened—here was his best chance of quietly leaving with no questions asked or answered. In their jug beside the bed the daisies had shed their flowers; he collected them from the floor, and arranged them in a circle on the table, looping the jug that had held them (the amber-haired girl would like that, he thought—Clare, had that been her name?—and for a moment regretted he'd never thanked her for her misplaced kindness). Then he lifted the lid of the child's desk and took the notebook from where he'd hidden it underneath a pile of yellowed newspapers, from some of which pictures and columns had been cut. He flicked through the pages, running his finger with surprise over the lines of neat blue handwriting—had he written all that, by the yellow light above the tower? He supposed he must have, and saw again the black-haired woman turning to face him, and felt the sensation of cold wine seeping through his shirt.

He turned to look once more behind him, then slipping the notebook into his pocket opened the door.

Barring his way as certainly as any gate, Clare stood in the dark hall, turning away from him toward the head of the staircase where sunlight flew its banners on the wall. She wore a man's white shirt that reached almost to her knees, and stood tiptoe on dirty bare feet as if ready to run at a moment's notice. She'd been playing with bindweed and twisted a few stems around her neck, and John suspected it had been done for an effect he refused to feel. When she heard the door open she turned and the weeds turned with her, regarding him with white eyes open. "*John.*" She whispered, but as a child might, so that it carried along the hall and would have woken anyone still sleeping; and what occurred to him first was that Elijah had sent for him.

"John—Eve says we need you and will you come *now* please." She shifted from foot to foot. "She says she needs you or needs someone and you'll do." When there was no immediate sign of obedience the girl tugged crossly at the bindweed as if someone else had put it there. "There isn't anyone else, is there? They've gone out for a while, and she said you'll do, and that you'd know."

The nausea, which had begun to recede, struck him again so forcibly that he leaned against the door frame for a moment, and pressed his forehead to the cool white-painted wood. *What now*, he thought, helpless against his sickness and the plea that creased her face with anxiety: what ought he to know—who was that other John, who ought to be standing where he stood now? And then, alongside the confusion, he felt a needling of resentment: oh, he would *do*, then, ever the last resort. He imagined her saying it, that black-haired laddish girl downstairs in whose eyes and voice he thought he'd detected mockery the night before, and in the end it was resentment and not the plea for help that roused him. Squaring his shoulders, and breathing hard to suppress the gorge rising sourly in his throat, he said: "Where shall I go then? What shall I do?"

She grinned in relief or surprise, and by way of answer dashed away from him and swung herself down the first step or two, calling over her shoulder, "Well, this way then, and hurry," as if it had been the beginning of a game. He moved after her, then remembering that he still held the notebook hastily returned it to the

drawer in the child's desk, regretting that after all he
could not take it with him.

When they reached the foot of the stairs the girl
paused with her hand on the banister and said, "I'm
going to go now. You'll know what to do." Then she
ran out into the garden through the narrow door at the
farthest end of the hall. It hung open a while on tired
hinges, showing a stretch of parched lawn and a glimpse
of the high mossy wall he'd first seen from the road.
John could not think what it was he ought to be doing,
or why she'd left him there, and might have followed
her had he not heard, from deep in the shadow cast
by the front door, a kind of low cry. It was not quite of
fear but of something more like denial, and then there
was another voice, and a name said softly several times
over: *Alex, Alex, Alex . . .*

As his eyes accustomed themselves to the hall's dim
air, he saw the young latecomer from the night before
crouching against the door and resting his head on
his forearms. He looked diminished, as though overnight he'd lost half his height and strength, and when
he raised his head his eyes were rimmed with shadow.
Beside him stood Eve, stooping to rest a hand on his
shoulder, her arm showing white against the dark fabric of his shirt. Neither acknowledged John, but talked

instead in low urgent murmurs, the young man gesturing toward the door as though he'd seen something slip out or come in. Then Eve turned to John and without speaking communicated a plea that conferred on him a responsibility and knowledge he neither felt nor understood. With a slight dip of her head, she gestured toward Alex, who'd drawn himself up a little and was picking at a graze on his knuckles with all the concentration of a craftsman. The movement plainly conveyed that John should do something, and that he would instinctively know what it was—she raised a hand toward him in mute appeal then passed it wearily over her forehead. Then she came toward him, put her mouth close to his ear and whispered: "Look, I'm sorry, it's your first day, I know—only I have tried, and Hester will be gone a while now—won't you have a word?" She drew away from him, and said—with delicacy, as if a boundary had been overstepped: "You understand. Don't you? That is, you *know* . . ." She paused, and he felt a moment's pleasure in seeing her disconcerted before the sensation of being entirely at a loss overwhelmed him. He began to protest, but the schoolboy stammer held his tongue, and before he could frame the words to keep them all at arm's length Alex stood, with a quick fluid motion wholly at odds with his defeated posture a moment before.

"Eve, look—it's John. Why didn't you say!" He cuffed at his eyes, and it was as if the rough gesture dislodged the misery and weariness that had weighed him down. Patting at his clothes, which were dusty from his huddling against the door, he came toward them, and landed a friendly blow on John's shoulder. Then he patted at the wall behind them, where a strip of paper unfurled from the damp plaster, and said vaguely, "I might go and have a snooze." He paused beside Eve, frowning as though he'd forgotten something, then briefly gripped her hand and said: "Yes, I think so," and slipped behind them into a room which John had not yet seen. As he did so a small brown envelope fell from his hand or pocket to the floor, and grateful for an excuse to conceal his confusion John stooped to pick it up. When he straightened, Eve had not followed the young man, but stood instead with folded arms, examining him as though he'd just arrived. She beckoned twice, imperious, and John passed her the envelope, noticing the stamp had not been franked. She folded it over and over as if she might eventually reduce it to nothing, and pushed it into her own pocket. "Shall we go? Clare has something to show you, I think." Then, with an authority that sat so curiously on her John could not have resisted it, she indicated that he should follow her down the hall and out into the garden.

It was early still and there ought to have been dew on the grass, but already the hard-baked earth had stored up the morning's sun and John felt it through the thin soles of his shoes. The forest pines huddled against the garden wall were shedding their needles to lighten their load, and up ahead an elm had been struck with disease so that half its branches were damned to perpetual winter. In the shade of the elm Clare in her white shirt knelt over a series of irregular white objects which might have fallen from the blighted elm. Drawing near, John saw they were a dozen small parcels wrapped in paper and tied with waxed string, several opened out and surrounded with scraps of paper in the long grass. Seeing Eve and John come toward her the girl snatched up a clay doll and shook its ugly little head to send them away. "You can't have her, she's mine!"

"I tell you the child never sleeps, up in the attic and down in the cellar at all hours, bringing out her treasures." Eve touched Clare's head with a fond gesture. "Last week it was a cannonball, of all things—it had been used as a doorstop in a room we never use, and she carried it out to the garden thinking it would make a bowling ball, and dropped it twice, and broke the floorboards on the way . . ." Then she fell to her knees, and tearing at a bundle of tissue withdrew a bundle of bamboo pipes set around a lacquered black dome. "What's this doing here, with these old things—isn't this mine? Didn't I have it last year?" She examined it, frowning, then pushed the black dome beneath her lower lip, and blowing over the pipes produced, without a thought, a line or two of Bach. *So it was her,* he thought, *at the piano last night, and in the morning.* He was disappointed, and would much rather it had been Hester making something fine and beautiful with her ugly hands.

Clare set the clay doll down in the grass, and covered it with a sheet of tissue paper, carefully leaving its upturned face exposed. Beside it lay a corked jar of yellow liquid in which a mouse or vole curled its pink hands and waved a naked tail. She said, with a shy eager smile, "I found them, all by myself, and brought them down while everyone was still in bed. Look!" She held up her wrist, which was looped three times with a string of irregular blue beads. "What do you think? Where do you think they came from?"

John stooped and tugged at the beads. He had seen something like it before, in a glass case or displayed on a cloth somewhere. "It might be tomb beads—from Egypt, you know. Nothing precious, just chips of glass—something to be buried with, so you don't go in poverty to the afterlife. Then in time all the sand blows away, and there they are, waiting to be picked up." He thought she might recoil, but instead she stroked them

thoughtfully, satisfied, and turned to a larger parcel, wrapped not in paper but in a length of chamois
leather. John, by an instinct for the familiar he later regretted, saw in the parcel the dimensions of a small book,
and felt the idea of leaving recede a little further. He
crouched beside her, and with a proprietorial murmur—
"Shall I, do you think?"—took it from her. The strings
came untied easily, as if it had been recently opened and
they'd lost the habit of their knot. Inside the chamois
was a second layer of frayed blue cloth, wrapped tightly
around the book's pale vellum binding. The gilding on
the spine had worn away, and John, setting the book
on his knees, turned to the title page. The thick paper
showed an engraving of a bearded man, splendidly aloof,
resting a long finger on a rolled parchment.

It was a volume which had come and gone from his
own shelves over the years—a collection of Anglo-Saxon
poems, inscrutable and lovely, the Old English and the
new shown on facing pages. The book's scent was so
familiar it conveyed the sound of the clock ticking in the
empty shop, and the bell above the door. The weight of
the book spread evenly between his palms gave him the
courage an icon might to a man of anxious faith.

Clare bent forward and traced a line or two with her
finger. "*Where is the horse gone,*" she read: "*Where
the rider . . .*"

"*. . . and where the giver of treasure . . .*" It gave John such pleasure to be back over the border of his own familiar land that he went on, eagerly, as if she'd asked to be taught: "No one knows now—might not have known then!—who was the rider, or where he rode, or even who wrote the poems. Their meaning is mine or yours; they belong to whoever reads them, and no one can say you are either right or wrong."

Eve, black brows drawn together in distaste, took the book. "*So spoke the wanderer, mindful of hardship.*" She snapped it shut, seeming again the boy he'd first taken her for. He laughed, and said, "Not all are so mournful, though most . . . This one I knew by heart when I was young, though I never knew what it meant: 'Wulf and Eadwacer—'" He stopped abruptly, remembering the notebook upstairs, and seeing in the sulphurous yellow light the name *EADWACER*, scrawled half a dozen times, and repeated on the deck of cards dealt out the night before. As he said the name the two young women kneeling on the grass paused, and looked up at him. Clare looked stricken, as though he'd said something to wound her, and Eve said sharply, "What? What did you say?"

Her hostility was so sudden and unearned it took great effort for him to say without stammering: "It was nothing—just another poem, that's all." He felt them begin to withdraw from him—Clare rocked back on her heels and crossed her arms against her breast, and Eve's narrow white face had become fixed and hostile.

"It was only the name of the poem. I don't even know if I'm saying it right . . ."

"Show me." Eve took the book, drawing quickly away from him. "*Wulf is on one island, I on another.*"

The obscure old riddle became part of everything else that was uncertain and troubling: he was still a stranger in their strange land. She said, "Why did you choose it—why did you have to say it out loud?"

"We've heard it before, you see, John," said Clare gravely. She looked, he thought, rather disappointed, and all at once older than her years.

"Yes." Eve began to wrap the book roughly, winding the string so tightly John flinched—*oh, but careful, you'll break its spine*—"Yes—everywhere, all over the house, cut into the table, written in dust on the windowsills. Down there"—Eve flung out an arm toward the high green bank at the garden's end.

"Down there?" John shielded his eyes from the sun at its height.

"Haven't you seen it yet? The reservoir." Oh, but it's a reservoir, of course, thought John—he'd seen that kind of embankment before on the outskirts of small towns where he and his brother fished without joy for trout and pike.

"We're going swimming there tomorrow," said Clare, forgetting for a moment the book and the hated name. The few tears she'd shed dried on her cheek. "We keep saying we'll go, but we never do."

"We might, darling," said Eve impatiently, not yet finished with John. Her eyes were opaque as smoked glass; then they cleared, suddenly, as though she had reached a favorable verdict on some fresh evidence. She shook her head. "Oh, how could you know? There have been"—she paused, as though selecting a word and finding it distasteful—"letters. Anonymous ones." She rolled her eyes. "Well, yes—you're smiling, and why wouldn't you. Absurd, isn't it? I keep thinking Holmes will arrive, with Watson following by train . . ."

"I wouldn't have thought so," said John. "Miss Marple, perhaps."

"It is more her line of work, isn't it?" The smoke receded, and left her mossy eyes clear and frank. "Poison pen letters. That's what they call them, as if it's not the person writing that's at fault but the pen in their hand—they come for Alex, of all people! You can imagine someone wanting to torment Walker, can't you." She said this with a slight secretive smile, which she swiftly shook off. "Or Hester, or even me. But Alex"—she shook her head. "Well—you know." John, who knew less now than he ever had, nodded.

"There's always something, with Alex. It was bridges before. This time it's the reservoir—he's got it into his head the dam will break, and the reservoir will burst the embankment, and the water will reach us down here. He says he sees it at night—he's standing on the front lawn and the sky turns black, and black water from the reservoir bursts out of all the windows and doors, taking all of us with it. I tell him every day it would need the Severn or the Thames to flood us here, even if there hadn't been a drought, even if the dam burst . . ." She shook her head, and unfolded a square of stained linen from its paper packet. It was embroidered with the text *THOU GOD SEEST ME*, and underneath the words a blue eye was coming unstitched. Eve picked at the trailing threads.

"Of course we don't argue or disagree with him, it would only make things worse, and besides, what do we know, about this dam or any other . . ."

John watched her refolding the linen square on her lap and saw, with a prick of anxiety, that the bluish-white skin above her knees was beginning to burn. "But surely—a disaster on that scale: it's unthinkable." He looked again at the raised grass bank; it seemed, in the curious brightness of its grass, more permanent than the house itself.

She shrugged. "There's a crack, he says, although

I've not seen it. Out he swims, when we're all in our beds, then comes and wakes me, with his hair dripping on my pillow, to tell me it's the width of his thumb, then the palm of his hand . . ." Kneeling between the scattered drawers, she spread her own hands hopelessly. "Then, a few weeks ago, just at the beginning of summer, down we came one morning and there were two letters for Alex, side by side on the doormat. Oh, he was pleased—no one writes anymore, do they? He thought a friend had found him. You know, from before." She said this tentatively, and again John had the curious feeling that she did so out of a delicacy for his own feelings, but could not think why. "Only they weren't letters, of course—just newspaper clippings, and all of them showed drownings, or floods. There was one with a terrible picture, from France, of two children who'd been stranded on a sandbank hunting for shells. They were lying on the sand, their hair all mixed up with the seaweed . . ." She shuddered. "On all the pieces of newspaper was that name again, Eadwacer—oh, how *do* you say it? Then it started turning up—scratched on the table, or written in pebbles down by the reservoir, or so he says—I've never seen it and of course, you never quite know."

The whole tale was so absurd, and at the same time so cruel, that John would have liked to laugh. The woman stood wearily. "It's all right," she said. "What could you say? What can any of us say? It's so *childish*. Once I even thought he was doing it, but he was never that way, not even—" And again she said: "*You* know, John. Not even then."

They think I'm in on something! he thought, and unwilling to risk her anger again said carefully, "But if the name's written down by the dam or on the patio then either it's one of you, or someone who comes here often."

"I know. And I don't know which would be worse. Isn't it odd," she said, smiling: "You turned up and I never for a minute thought it might be you, though even as strangers go, you're fairly strange." Much later John was to remember that phrase, and wonder why it had felt so like an unexpected touch on the arm. Pressing her hands to the dip in her spine and turning her face to the sun she said, "Let's not talk about it anymore." Then she ran to peer at the shadow on the broken sundial, swore beneath her breath and vanished into the cool dark house. Clare stood, examining a bitten-down thumbnail, while the sound of a piano played in intricate swift patterns reached them across the lawn.

"How did she know the time," said John, "when the sundial's broken?"

"It doesn't matter, does it? It tells the same wrong time every day."

The music sank into a deep murmur felt as much as heard.

"Have you been friends with Eve a very long time?" John unbuttoned his cuff, and let the girl stoop to wrap the string of beads around his wrist.

"She's not my friend, not really. She knew my brother from school. I didn't see her for years, not for years, then she came to St. Jude's and of course we saw her all the time then, sometimes every day."

"I see," said John. St. Jude's? The image of Eve's black head bent over folded hands vanished as soon as it came. From across the lawn the patterns of music changed to an insistent motif that made him uneasy. "She's very good," he said, though really he couldn't tell.

"See, they suit you—yes, they say she is, and if she makes a mistake she slams the lid so hard you'd think she'd smash it in pieces. Did you know it was Eve who found the piano at St. Jude's—it was old and damp and none of the notes would come out right—but she paid to have it fixed. Alex liked to hear it." She gave him a curious look that was, he thought, half-pitying: "Of course everyone did."

Did she feel pity for him, then—for the man who should've been there, kneeling on the lawn with his wrist in her hands? The idea baffled him, and he put it away to examine later by a better light. Then she fastened the beads and said, "You know, sometimes she plays so long her fingers bleed. You can't go near her now, not until she's done."

"I promise I'll never disturb her," said John, remembering how quickly her mossy eyes had darkened. "I wouldn't like to make her angry. Listen: isn't someone calling for you?"

At the kitchen window, almost hidden by the half-closed blind, Hester beckoned the girl indoors, and dropping the blue beads in the grass she dashed away, forgetting him as easily as a child might.

He retreated into the strip of shade thrown by the high walls that divided the garden from the road, imagining an iron gate set within the bricks, its lock and hinges choked with ivy. *I've wondered enough at what I have done,* he thought, *but what have they done; what keeps them here, pleasure or punishment . . .* "Still no birds, then?" Alex had come quietly on bare feet and stood smiling at him, his hands deep in his pockets, nothing like the frightened boy crouching by the door he'd seen that morning. His skin had tanned so darkly the long-fringed eyes appeared pale.

"No, none; it's like this in London—just as I left I saw one dying in the gutter—I thought here it would be different."

"London, eh?" The younger man looked surprised.

Then he shrugged, and said: "Makes you wonder where they've all gone, doesn't it? But it can't last—nothing ever does . . . John, I want to say something." He flushed, as though he thought he might be speaking out of turn and, forestalling a response, went on: "I know what it takes just to leave everything, not to do what they tell you to do, but you're not on your own. And I'll help you, if I can—oh, you don't want to talk about it, I understand."

John, wretched with confusion and guilt, said, "You're very kind." Casting about for a means of moving the subject to firmer ground, he gestured to the packets scattered on the lawn. "Ought we to take these in?" He took up the book and concealed it beneath his arm. The young man stooped obediently and began to gather up what remained, now and then exclaiming, "What *is* all this, anyway? And where did she find them? Let's take them to the red room, and find a home for them there."

Singing under his breath something that echoed by chance or design the melody that reached them across the lawn, he led John toward the house and a glass door which stood open at the edge of the stone terrace. Pausing at the threshold John saw a piano with its lid raised and a dark head bent low over the keys; remembering his resolve not to trouble Eve he slipped quietly inside.

It was a larger room than any he'd seen in the house before. It ran the length of the east wing so that all along the outer wall eight windows faced south to the gray-paved terrace, then to the parched lawn and the dark pines beyond. The light that came in ought to have blazed in every corner, but instead was absorbed by red-papered walls and Turkish carpets scattered unevenly across the wooden floor. The ceiling seemed lower than in the other rooms, and had been recently painted with illogical pairings of spring flowers and roses, and all around the light fittings, from which hung broken chandeliers trailing chipped strings of glass drops, were painted yellow-beaked blackbirds caught in a briar thicket. The furniture was set around the piano, which was by far the largest John had ever seen, and bore no resemblance to the comfortably scuffed wooden instrument his brother's children played. It seemed newly made, lacquered to so black and lucid a shine that he saw in its raised lid a perfect dark reflection of himself at midnight. The keys were not ebony and bone but plastic, with a fine strip of scarlet felt running behind them. The harsh colors in the dim and shabby room reminded John of false teeth bared in a grin. Scattered all around the piano were piles of sheet music, some of it torn and foxed with illuminated title pages, others on clean white paper. Elsewhere the furniture was desperately shabby: a velvet-upholstered couch was balding in the seat, and the pair of tables set between the windows looked as if they had rickets. All around the room, stuffed into vases and jugs and attracting a number of voluble bees, were stems of untidy long-petaled red and yellow flowers, their hard stamens ejecting puffs of dark pollen. It looked as if someone had set a dozen small fires, and they smelled revoltingly sweet.

"Asphodel, she calls them," said Eve drily, closing the piano lid. "Lilies, to you and me."

Alex laid his armful of packages in a neat row on the seat of a couch. He looked up at the girl, who returned his gaze with a searching, anxious look of her own which swiftly became a smile. "I'm done, I think, for now—where's Walker? Have you seen him?" Standing half-hidden in the curtain's musty folds John saw Alex lift her hand and examine it, turning it over and putting his thumb in her palm. "Don't you ever wash, Evie?" he said gently. "Look at all this, under your nails." He let her hand drop, and then he said: "I haven't seen him this morning. He's probably up with Elijah, leading him astray. Yesterday he was teaching him to gamble, you know . . ." The woman laughed, then pushed her curls back from her forehead, waved distractedly at them both, and went out into the hall.

The young man watched her go, scratching at a raised mosquito bite on his arm; then he shook his head and, seeing John, started as if he'd forgotten he was there. "I can't stand this much longer," he said. "Still, we'll all be out of it, come Saturday."

John glanced behind him out of the window, expecting to see clouds pulling at the sun, but there was only the same empty blue canopy. "Oh?"

"Didn't they tell you? We're getting out of here, going to the sea. Won't you come too?"

"Of course," said John. How easy it would be to leave them then, with none of those inept excuses he'd dreamed up in the night. He imagined pushing open the door to his flat, and seeing inside the rush mat with three pairs of shoes neatly paired alongside, and the bookshelves as ordered as those in the shop. He awaited relief and longing for home, but neither came.

"It can get a bit closed-in here sometimes," said the younger man suddenly, sitting up and grasping the arms of the chair: "Nice to have another face—another pair of eyes, if you see what I mean." He looked at John with such warmth and gratitude that he flushed, and stooped to pick uselessly at a shoelace. Then Alex said, worrying at a graze on the back of his hand: "I don't think I did know you, back then, did I?" His eyes met

John's, and for a moment he was the huddled wretched boy he'd been that morning.

"Oh no, no. No—I don't think so, I'm sure I'd remember."

"Only you see I am sometimes—sometimes not always clear . . ." The graze evidently became sore; he winced, and rested his head on the arm of the chair. "But here it feels safe, as if nothing can make it through the forest to where we are. Do you see?"

"I think so."

"Listen," he said, standing. "Would you help me with something?"

"If I can, of course."

"I could do with a hand, later. Down by the reservoir." He looked anxious, and John remembered the tale Eve told, and saw that name again, with its familiar syllables: *Eadwacer*, written in the notebook upstairs and scratched into the wood on the kitchen table, and perhaps in other places waiting to be discovered.

"If you think I can be of any use," he said.

"Can you swim?"

"I'm not sure," said John: "I can't remember."

"It won't matter—was that Hester calling us to lunch?" He put a hand on John's shoulder where the shirt was damp with sweat growing stale, and said: "You've probably got time to change."

Dear Jon (may I call you Jon?),

Last night I slept in your bed, and this morning I put on your clothes. I took them from one of the bags you left here: I hope you don't mind. I'm sure they're all wondering what a man like me is doing in a red tartan shirt with sleeves too short by an inch.

"A man like me," I said; but the point is that I must be a man like you—I must be you, and put you on when I put on these jeans (which I notice are not clean and have about them a smell a little like smoke and a little like the lawn outside, where all the grass has died).

I've kept a record of what I've done and said in your name. Don't be alarmed—I've done no harm, though I've done what I ought not to have done, and left undone those things which I ought to have done . . .

I've been through your bags, and this is what I found:

A biology textbook, hardly read.
A joke set of plastic false teeth with pink feet attached.

Two bottles of clear nail varnish.

A Book of Common Prayer (marked with
Elijah's name, and an address scratched out).

Four white porcelain dolls' hands, and a plastic
doll's leg.

A prescription for antihistamines made out to a
Mr. Williams.

A bottle of lavender oil (empty).

Five steel bolts, very clean.

A thin glove packed with gauze.

A glass eye.

Actually, the glass eye was in the pocket of these jeans. I thought perhaps you collected marbles, and found myself rolling it between my finger and thumb, wondering if you did the same for comfort's sake. When I took it out just now and saw the green pupil and the bloodshot white I half expected it to blink, so I put it back in my pocket to protect it from the light.

Who are you—who are we? What did we all do that brought us here? I only know they can't ever have seen you, or even heard your voice—when we spoke on the phone you had an accent I couldn't place that was nothing like mine.

Who are you, Jon? And what are you doing with these things—that glove you could mistake for a severed hand, the limbs of a doll, the teeth you must've found in a joke shop on a pier? Carry on like this and you'll have enough to make yourself a whole new man.

I'd guess that you're young, and as troubled as they all seem to be. You're shorter than I am and stockier too, and from what I've seen on your collar I imagine your hair could do with a cut. And you're a thief, with the names of other men on your books and papers—is the textbook even yours? What was it you wanted to know—was there no one to ask? You've read the prayer book—I can see that— Elijah would never have folded down the pages till the paper cracked. And I can see the page you've read most, because you touched the paper too often with dirty hands—"You have placed in the skies the sign of your covenant with all living things . . ." (and I'm not a religious man but I know a rainbow when I see one).

I know what you're thinking. I've no right to your clothes or your name or your place at their table. But read what I've written and you'll see: they took my arm—they touched me and wanted me here . . .

Oh, but it's useless I know. Soon enough they'll catch me out and besides, it was never me they wanted.

Keep this book safe, would you? *Please do that.*

Yours,

John Cole

II

Later, when a too-heavy lunch had been eaten, and doors closed one after the other upstairs as the afternoon torpor settled on the house, John walked alone in the garden. The letter—torn from the notebook and placed under the painted Puritan's frame—ought to have shaken him loose, but seemed instead to fix him in place. As he walked across the dying lawn he cast about for sight of Eve walking between the poplars or Hester at her window, already feeling it his duty now to observe, if not take part. He rolled the glass eye across his palm; there was the dying elm, and there the raised bright bank of the reservoir, but nothing moved—no shadow on the grass, or shiver in the branches overhead. There also, of course—he'd never thought to look!—would be the narrow track down which he'd walked, and beyond it the long road home. He stood sunstruck alone on the lawn—*I can go I must go I will*—then thought suddenly of the notebook upstairs. He imagined Clare finding it one early morning as she ranged about the house, passing it between them all, reading it aloud.

He turned back, to the gray-paved terrace and its broken sundial, and the roses dying in their beds. Upstairs a window was opened and the sun slid across the pane; a note or two was struck on the piano, but nothing came of it. John crossed the threshold to the blue room where he'd sat in silence the night before, feeling the glass eye grow hot in his palm, and gave a shameful cry of surprise as a hand emerged from a dim corner and beckoned him farther in. Elijah, holding a glass of water in which floated an opaque ice cube cracking as it melted, gestured toward an empty chair. The gentle invitation had the proportions of a threat (*I think we'd better have a talk*): John started guiltily, and dropped the eye, which made its way across the carpet, settled against the leg of an armchair, and fixed its gaze upon the ceiling.

"John!" It was clear he'd been waiting. "John! That is to say . . ." Delicately, by little more than a raised eyebrow, he put out the question which John had dreaded and longed for.

"Oh no—I *am* John. You see, that's been my trouble!"

"Care to tell me about it? I've kept a good many secrets"—the preacher pulled, wincing, at the iced water—"not *all* of them mine."

"It was just a mistake," said John. "I didn't mean to do it." The plaintive note in his voice was new and unwelcome, and flushing miserably he wished the arms of the chair would draw him in until he seeped into the wood.

"So easily done," said the other man, benevolently. "Wide is the gate, and broad is the way . . ." He paused, then thinking better of the turn he'd taken said: "You came in last night so pale, and seemed so weary, that it didn't much matter that you weren't the Jon I knew. Certainly you looked as though you belonged here— what right did I have to turn you out?"

"Does everyone know?" Appalled, John considered the possibility that all their welcome had been an act of amused pity. The glass eye rolled his way in sympathy.

"Oh, no! No, they never knew the lad—he was one of mine, if you take my meaning, and fetched up at St. Jude's a while back, following his pastor like a dutiful member of the flock. A tendency to a particular kind of kleptomania, I'm given to understand. Harmless, but one never knows where these things lead. In my day we sang with the children '*Little* sins become *big* sins, and *big* sins *kill*'—just like that, can you imagine—*big sins kill!*"

"I've no right to ask you, I know—but I'd like to understand at least what I've seen and heard since I came—what is St. Jude's? What does it mean? I thought at first of a church but can't seem to make it fit."

"Ah . . ." There was another of those slight changes of air, and Elijah sat a little straighter. He pursed his mouth in a gesture of distaste, drained his glass, and set it down. "Not a church, or not quite: a private hospital, a—what do they call it these days?—a psychiatric hospital, a convalescent home, an institute, a retreat. I was there first, biding my time, waiting for it all to pass. Quiet it was, at first; routine, order, soft-soled shoes. Then Alex came, not in his right mind. There'd never been anyone quite like him before, not in my time at least. A deep sadness in him, an anger even; they couldn't contain it at first. And then the women came— I remember thinking it was like Mary visiting Christ in his tomb. Hester first, with Clare always at her side, and not long after that Eve also, though she looked so different then, and wore her hair so long she could wrap it round her like a scarf."

"Months ago? Years ago—weeks?"

"I don't remember. Autumn was coming—a year ago, I suppose. Then Walker came—something to do with the finance of the place; I never asked. And something altered, and in the end every boundary was crossed, every mark was overstepped, and we all left together—Alex, Clare, Eve and me. It was Hester's doing, as things so often are. It's a lonely place this, with all the rooms empty, and she told them, 'Send others, if they need it; if they're not ready to be alone.' Between you and me, I think she'd hit on a way of saving her soul. But no one ever came, and we never mentioned St. Jude's again. Then a month ago I took a call from Jon, and said: do come, do. There's no harm in coming here."

He shook his head, and left a quiet opening into which John—leaning forward, imagining a confessional grille suspended in the air between them—put all the events of the day before. Elijah greeted the tale without surprise or censure, nodding now and then, and murmuring, "Yes, I see" or "Yes, quite so"; and when John had finished he said, "I consider it none of my business whatever. Stay or go as you please, and I'll say nothing. If asked, well—I can try my hand at a lie."

Muddy with heat, John stirred in his chair; a new thought had come to him, and with great difficulty he forced it onto his tongue. "Then—is this why no one ever asks me where I came from, or what I'm doing here?"

Elijah, standing with a groan, gave a smile of mischief and delight. "Oh, they think you came from there too. They all just assumed you were mad."

III

It's very late or very early, depending, which way up you hold the day, and I've been down at the reservoir with Alex. He told me to wait for him after we'd eaten, and I sat till after midnight on the terrace, drinking the coffee Hester gave me (she makes it bitterly thick—no wonder I can't sleep), watching bats come over the wall from the forest and listening to Eve play in the room behind me. She'd opened the windows wide and I could smell the lilies dying in their vases. By then the heat had made everyone tired and listless and no one seemed to feel much like talking. Mostly they left me alone, although once someone put their hand on my shoulder on their way down through the trees. Clare sat cross-legged next to me for a long time, showing me how to blow a blade of grass like an oboe reed. I pretended I didn't know how, and let her teach me, all the while thinking: tomorrow I'll leave and be forgotten by the time the weather breaks.

Behind us Walker paced up and down smoking so heavily it looked as though autumn had come and he was walking through morning mist. Elijah came to the window once or twice and looked down toward the yellow light by the reservoir as if he wanted to go down, but was terrified of what he'd find. I wonder what frightens him? Watching him there at the window I thought it must be something he sees that passes the rest of us by.

The chair I'd carried out was too old and worn in the seat to be comfortable, but all the same I dozed off twice, my chin on my chest and the back of my neck stretched as if it would break. Behind me Eve went on playing, breaking off sometimes to swear quietly but viciously, and play a dozen times the phrase she'd mistaken, until the memory of it must have lodged in all the bones and tendons of her hands. The same phrases over and over seemed to give me a kind of clarity—I remembered the poem I'd seen that morning as clearly as if I had memorized it yesterday, or years ago perhaps when I was young, and my mind held on to things. I recited the lines to myself, making them fit with the phrases she played . . . Wulf is on one island, I on another, Wulf is on one island, I on another . . . Then Alex came and woke me with a thump between my shoulders so hard it nearly threw me out of my chair.

He said, "Sorry to keep you, John—shall we go?" and crooked out his arm toward me. I took it, and it wasn't until we'd gone a little farther on I realized no one had walked with me like that since I'd last seen my brother. He's shorter than Christopher, and his arm was slender but strong. He said, "It's good of you, you know. I don't like asking the others. Clare's afraid of the water at night—she thinks drowned men will come up and get her by the ankles. Have you been down and seen it yet?"

I said I hadn't, and he squeezed my arm.

"It's not much of a reservoir, really. We get our water from there, and so do the villages between here and the coast road, but no more than that. You've seen the valve tower?"

"Is that what it is? I can see the light from my window. It doesn't look like it belongs here."

"I hate the light. It keeps me awake and turns my skin yellow like a man that's been poisoned . . . I've told Hester I can go down and take out the bulb, but she says she likes it, like a midnight sun—as if we haven't had enough sun by now!"

We walked slowly down toward the light, and as we

left the house behind, the hard earth became springy and pliable underfoot. As we drew nearer to the rough land beyond the garden I could make out white patches on the earth, like smears of drying saltwater. While we walked he told me more about the reservoir, quite contentedly, not at all as if he dreaded the water breaching the dam and reaching us where we stood. I wondered if Eve had been teasing me that morning as we sat under the dying elm, and felt suddenly very relieved. The whole business of the letters had been so childish and inane that I was glad I didn't have to believe it after all. Alex went on talking, and I remember thinking how like his sister's his voice was, cheerful and childlike and not much bothered whether or not I was listening, or had much to say in reply.

He told me the reservoir was made before the war by flooding a hamlet that had once been within view of the house. The dam had stopped up a river so narrow no one had really believed it would rise to cover the post office and chapel, and the dozen cottages clinging to the single road. There were no protests, he told me—no one had much cared about the chapel, which had been used by a sect called the Particular People, famous for praying out of doors. Elderly couples in the cottages were only too glad to move to new apartments with neat kitchens and a supervisor who'd come if they had a fall on the doorstep. Only the postmistress had taken it badly, hoarding letters in their sacks for weeks so they were never delivered, and were dislodged when the water came. For a long time after, he said anyone passing by would have seen white envelopes floating on the black water.

"About a week ago the water got just low enough to see the post office sign. When we get there, tell me if you can see it."

I asked him about the valve tower, and who came there. We'd drawn near it by then, and its yellow light gave him a hard translucent look as if he were made of amber. The tower was smaller than it had looked from the window, with red bricks neatly set in a checkered pattern, and a crenellated roof. The door was sheet metal, secured with rivets and heavily padlocked, but I could see through a grimy window to a mechanism studded with dials, and a computer with a dusty screen. A laminated sheet of paper stained with damp had been taped to the door. It said NO ENTRY.

"It's supposed to regulate the flow of water from the dam," he told me. "They come once or twice a year, maybe more. I never see them." Then his arm through mine tensed suddenly. He lowered his voice to a whisper, although there was no one near who might have heard. "I tried to call them. I did. There's a number on the door. Yesterday I called and the day before, and twice this morning before anyone was up, but they won't listen. They said they'd send someone this month, maybe next, but it might be too late by then—the summer's ending and there'll be rain for days." We'd reached the place where the parched lawn gave way to gravel and rough grass, and banks of bramble with berries dying unripe between the leaves. The brambles had put out low branches that crept across the ground and caught our ankles as we passed.

We came to the cannonball Eve told me had been brought down from the attic—it must have been found on a tide line somewhere, and was crusted with barnacles and rust. Alex bent to pick it up, holding it out to me cupped between his hands, laughing and hefting it from side to side as though he wanted me to see how strong he was. He carried it a few feet, pretending to toss it in the air like a tennis ball, but I could see how the weight of it raised ridges of muscle and tendon in his arm, and when he dropped it I thought I'd hear it ring like a ship's bell on the hard earth. I looked at Alex, who'd stopped suddenly when he dropped the cannonball, and was staring fixedly at the embankment. It was only ten or fifteen feet high, on a sharp slope he could've dashed up without losing his breath or footing, but he looked for a moment old and defeated. He started plucking feverishly at the skin on his bottom lip, leaving a smear of blood. I walked past him and said loudly, "I'll beat you to the top." It was childish of me, but it worked—he laughed and overtook me, and I reached the crest of the embankment a moment after him.

We stood together on the high grass verge, the valve tower throwing its light on the dwindling reservoir. The waterline must once have been almost level with the grass embankment, but had receded in the drought and left a kind of rough beach littered with feathers and algae. All around us the dark pines of the forest stooped toward the water as if they were thirsty. I'd grown so used to parched lawns and dying flower beds that the few spikes of purple foxglove growing near the water's edge seemed strange and rare, and I looked down at my feet afraid I might trample them into the ground. Alex swept out a hand to take in the reservoir from where we stood to the dam wall in the distance. "What do you think?"

It was smaller than I'd thought, and darker. The surface of the water was black and opaque, and the reflection of the moon at our feet looked very small. He beckoned me nearer the edge, asking if I could see the post office sign, and I stepped forward until I was almost on the rubble beach. The pupils of my eyes opened to the dark until I could make out, just below the thick water, the familiar red oval.

He told me how he liked to go there alone, watching for waterfowl. One day he'd seen a pair of geese that looked as though their breasts had been painted red, and had never seen them again. There'd been kingfishers, and once an adder he'd known by the diamonds on its back. He pointed out the pine where he thought he'd heard a cuckoo. ("Just like the clock!" he told me, although I don't see why that would be a surprise.) Then he turned his back to the dam as though he wanted to put it out of his mind, and in his rush to tell me everything he'd seen—mayflies mating on the water, and a vole lying dead with its tail in its mouth—he began to swallow and stumble over his words until I couldn't follow what he was saying.

All the things I'd heard that morning came back to me—the letters, the flawed dam and the water ready to rise; St. Jude's and everything Elijah had said; Eve playing to people I pictured leaning on white-painted walls to listen. I saw also the many versions of Alex I'd watched throughout the day: huddled by the front door, or asking for my help as easily as if we'd been friends for years. Looking at him then, as he stood linking his thumbs and flapping his joined hands, imitating a white moth he'd seen the night before, it suddenly seemed obvious that he was suffering in ways I couldn't describe or understand.

I found myself nodding and saying, "Yes, yes, I see," and moving back from the water's edge. Then, without pausing for breath, he tilted back his head to look at the sky, and said, "I think that's the Pole Star, isn't it? Elijah taught me how to find it once—look, you follow the line of the W, I forget what it's called—yes, it's the Pole Star right enough." Then he looked back at me, and it was as if locating that single point had steadied him, as though it were not something distant at all, but a bright shaft that pinioned him safely by my side. He frowned and shook his head, knuckling at his eyes like someone who'd just woken from a brief sleep. When I told him that he was right, and that every day it is there too, though we can't see its modest light when the sun's nearby, he gave me one of his frank childlike smiles and immediately I thought I must be wrong, and that I'd mistaken nothing but a harmless preoccupation for lunacy—it was as steady and direct a smile as I'd ever seen. Then he said, "Anyway, I'd like your help. Can you swim?"

When I told him I'd really rather not in that dark water he laughed and said, "Fair enough," and told me he only did it now that he knew the water so well he could have swum there blindfolded. He stooped to unlace his sneakers, and I asked him why it was he needed to go out there at all. I tried to sound as if I didn't care, and he didn't look up but said casually, as if I probably knew already, "Oh, I like to check at midnight, you see. No sense checking in the morning then leaving it all day—anything could happen at night, don't you think?"

Then he took off his socks, pushed them into the toes of his sneakers, and began to stoop and stretch like an athlete before a race. Between deep breaths he told me why he wanted to swim out into the black water.

He'd sat one day on the embankment wall reading a letter when he saw a bird fly up from near the center of the dam. From its forked tail he'd thought it was a swift, but when later that night he'd looked it up he knew from its pale breast it must have been a house martin. For a few days he watched for it, and saw the same bird go to and from the dam early in the morning, and again at sunset. He could never make out where it had been going, but often it had a scrap of something in its beak— a piece of bark or blade of dying grass, and once a white fragment torn from a pillow or cushion—and he knew that somewhere it must have made itself a home in a cleft in the reservoir wall.

"Everyone knows, don't they, how house martins make their nests in houses or barns—anywhere they find a place," he said. "But it was a long time before I knew what it meant, although now it seems so obvious—yes, yes: you thought of it right away, didn't you, I can tell! Somewhere there must be a hole or crack, just big enough for the bird to be making its nest, growing wider and longer every day while we all sit down there in the garden. But even then I didn't see it. I was slow, always have been, but now I understand, now I know what's coming. They say a storm's on its way, and the water will rise and—oh," he stopped and put his hand on my shoulder and said, smiling, "I don't need to tell you, do I, it's so obvious—it'll go into the crack and force it open, and then . . ." He waved savagely toward the reservoir then swept his arm down toward the house, and I imagined that after it he brought a hundred thousand gallons of dirty water. "Hester, Elijah, Walker, Evie, Clare," he said, as if he were seeing them all going under.

With every name he pressed my shoulder until it hurt, then suddenly he let go and took off his T-shirt. I remember turning away out of decency and confusion, then remembering that he also was a man and turning back. He was sunburned on his neck and forearms, and elsewhere his skin was pale as Eve's—it looked in the dark as though he were dressed in white. When he turned away from me I saw, on his upper arm where a muscle dipped as he moved, a patch of darker skin the size of my palm, as though he were always accompanied by a small shadow. Then he dropped the shirt and looked out over the water. "It's all right, I won't be long," he said kindly, and I realized I must have looked apprehensive, and tried to pin up a smile. He said, "It takes me sixteen minutes—I know because I timed it. Four to swim there and four back, and a little while to see what's happening."

He dropped the rest of his clothes in the dust, and I was so anxious to help, and so unsure of what I should do, that I picked them up and began to fold them over my arm. His T-shirt had picked up burrs from the weeds growing thickly on the bank, and I tugged them free from the folds of cloth and tossed them into the water. He said, "I haven't found it yet—the place where the dam's breaking. But as the water level gets lower and lower, I stand more chance of finding it, you see, and then"—he nodded toward the valve tower—"then they'll have to come, won't they?"

I've always thought people look diminished and vulnerable without their clothes, but Alex was so unselfconscious that he seemed to grow taller and broader as he stood there. He seemed to search my face for something—I don't know what, or I'd have given it to him—then said again, "They will come, John, won't they? When I tell them?" Of course I didn't know, though I doubted it—I was tired and hot, and the headache that had plagued me since I'd woken on the floor in my own room a hundred years ago was beginning to blind me again. I'd've said anything, I think, to avoid his gaze and go back to the iron bed upstairs, and draw the curtains against the sickly valve tower light. So I nodded and said, "I imagine they'd have to. If you had the proof." Then I immediately felt ashamed of myself and plucked another burr from the clothes I held—I knew I should reason with him, but I knew also that I was an imposter, and had no part in whatever they all chose to do. The young man's face suddenly changed (it's a trick they all have, I've noticed, of changing face like a tossed coin), and he gave me one of the frank childlike smiles that made me think he was saner than all of us.

"Knew I could count on you," he said triumphantly. "Knew it! You see"—he leaned toward me and I could smell stale beer and meat on his breath—"I don't know if they really believe me." He nodded ruefully toward the house. "They think I'm being a bit, you know." He tapped his forehead, and we both laughed.

As I remember it now I think how mad we both must have looked: Alex naked and at ease, idly batting away a fly drawn to his sweat, and me a little distance away fussing over an armful of clothes. I did what was easiest—I laughed with him, and tapped my own forehead too, and said, "No one could think that, not really. Not if you told them everything you've told me." I let him think nothing could be more logical than for him to pick his way on bare feet across the rubble beach toward the black water.

The moon and the yellow light from the tower gave enough brightness for me to see him dwindle until the dark water reached his waist, then he struck out for the dam wall. He called out to me once, then after that it was so quiet I could hear the swift splashes of his arms cutting through the water. A moment later and there was nothing, although I think I heard him call again from somewhere away to my right.

I don't know how long I waited. Perhaps he really had timed how long the task took, but it seemed to me that the moon moved across the sky and back while I walked up and down at the foot of the slope. Once or twice the yellow light flickered violently and I thought the bulb would blow—that I'd be left alone in the dark, and he'd have nothing to guide him out of the water— but it always came back and sent my shadow across the lawn toward the house. By the time he climbed silently out of the water I was tired and distracted, and when I felt his wet hand on my shoulder I thought for a moment the drowned men Clare was afraid of had found me out.

He said, "Nothing tonight, I'm afraid—nothing to see." He patted my back, as if he thought I'd be disappointed too. "It's all right, we can check tomorrow, can't we, now we both know what we've got on our hands? Makes a difference to me, I can tell you, knowing you believe me—I'll sleep better tonight." He grinned, took his clothes from me and quickly dressed. "You look awful," he said. "Let's get you home." And because it was so ridiculous, finding myself being kindly led indoors by a half-naked boy, still wet from swimming at night to find a place underwater where birds might nest, I began to laugh and, as though it were contagious, he did too. By the time we reached the house we were both laughing, until we gasped for breath and clutched at each other's arms as we walked.

At the foot of the stairs he said, "I'll leave you now—I won't sleep for a long while," and turned toward the kitchen. His feet left black prints on the flagstones. Then he turned back and said, shyly and as though he were afraid he might have transgressed, "Sometimes I forget where I've been and what I've done, so you see I don't like to be alone . . . Tonight while I was in the water I thought, I can feel it on my back, and I can hear it splashing, and John is there waiting, and if he is there, so must I be too . . ." Then he plunged forward, with the same motion as when he had struck out into the water, and squeezed my shoulder so hard that I have the marks of his hand on me now. Then Hester called him from the kitchen and I came upstairs alone.

IV

Hester watched their return across the lawn. The yellow light from the reservoir gave each man a kind of aura, and it was impossible to tell from that distance who was supporting whom, only that every few steps one would stagger a little with laughter or weariness and be tugged to his feet again. She drew the curtains, not wanting to be seen, and sat at the dining table rolling the glass eye back and forth across the wood. She felt rather sorry for it, with the white clouded and bloodshot, and the hazel-streaked iris turning uselessly this way and that. The house closed about her like a clam shell; it was the hour she liked best, with all her duties done. She numbered her guests one by one on her fingers, a tally of the day's work: Eve, Clare, Alex (impossible to prevent a smile at the name), Eli-

jah, John—she lightly touched the eye and imagined it
blinking, hurt.

That rash promise the year before, just as the door to
St. Jude's had closed behind them, had been sincerely
meant. She'd felt a sudden urge to fill each room, remembering long years in which she longed to hear
a door slam or the piano played. There'd been times
when even an intruder would have been a welcome
sight; she'd have opened up her jewelry box (truth be
told, all those pretty things were never worn), and put
the kettle on.

But once they'd come together through the forest—
Alex mute, she remembered, curled in the back of her
car with his knees to his chest—and taken up their resi-
dence, the promise had been quickly forgotten in a kind
of collective act: better to think they'd always been there.
She found herself growing deliberately vague about
the house and its origins (oh, a family estate—a kind
of inheritance, she supposed: unexpected, unwanted,
a burden in many ways; but so good to be *useful*) and
sometimes indulged in a little mythmaking—she was
born there; she'd found it one morning out walking;
she'd broken in and never left.

Elijah's tentative reminder of her promise, and his
plea for the inclusion of the man he'd known before he'd
parted ways with God, had been at first resented. Her

protective impulse had grown stronger with every week that passed, until she came to think of it as exerting a power of restraint (*they cannot leave me*, she'd once said aloud). An outsider might break the bond; but she'd given her word and that was that. Odd, though—she picked up the glass eye and popped it in her mouth— she'd imagined him to be a younger man, a boy almost, and had been startled at the appearance of that tall grave man with the beard that grew rather thinly around his mouth, giving his face a vulnerable and sensual cast of which, she was certain, he was quite unaware.

She had felt also the effect on him of her own appearance, but was so accustomed by now to evoking a mix of pity and distaste that it hardly troubled her. It was a hard-won indifference, though she still remembered the painful realization that she was unfit for the male attention her sister enjoyed (it was the same sister, encountering her once in the bath, who'd first alerted her to her own ugliness, by loudly recoiling from her too-fat thighs showing above the foam and going away laughing, the bathroom door open, so that Hester had to cross the room naked and ashamed to hide herself again).

It was not in her nature to avoid her faults, and so she took to a minute examination and cataloging of them: the preposterous nose; the coarse skin, in which the pores seemed to grow larger over time; the tendency to spots and boils; the pendulous flesh on her arms; and the weight of her breasts and stomach, which pulled at the small of her back and made it ache. In time her shame had hardened into a kind of defiance; what God had taken away from her body he'd given abundantly elsewhere. No one would look twice at her, it was true—but nor would they outthink her, outwit her, forget her, or cause her a moment's unease. By the time she entered drama school ("I daresay you'll get a lot of *character parts*") she outate and outdrank her companions, Falstaff in jet beads and high-laced boots. She was uniformly tolerated and frequently liked, and being both above and beneath suspicion was permitted friendships with men that might otherwise have been forbidden.

She taught herself to care nothing for the love she believed her body excluded, rejoicing at weddings while hardening herself against any expectation that she might one day wear the little gold seal of possession.

The hardening was not immediate or complete: there'd been, of course, a loved one, though she could not have said what fixed her affection on him, only that in his presence she felt elated and miserable all at once.

That he openly enjoyed her company with an uncomplicated friendliness was so much the worse; she was a foil to his humor, which was not always kind, and at times the authority which was the compensation for her failure ever to be girlish was all that kept him in check. And being above and beneath suspicion, they often shared a room, to the amusement of his careless lovers ("Oh, Hester, do see he behaves!"). There was a night when she lay awake on the floor (not admitting that the offered bed was too narrow), and listening to his restless movements heard *Hester, come here I need you*, but feeling the shame of her body lay in silence. The thing was that he rarely remembered by morning what was done at night half-sleeping, and would not have known whether she'd kept her place on the floor, or come to stoop over him and put herself to his mouth, which is what he would have asked her to do.

She was no success on the stage, and blamed her appearance quite cheerfully, since the truth (she could not act) was far worse. It was easy then to retreat to the house with its dark places and curious yellow light, and welcome friends who'd come for a day and remained, enchanted, for a week. There came a time of enormous popularity, when her height and heaviness became cause for admiration, perfectly suited to her place at the head of the table. Clare and Alex, to whom she'd once laughingly refused to be godmother ("I can't help but feel He's never been *entirely* on my side . . ."), were the remnants of that time in which she was half-hostess, half-servant, developing the lasting role which she now had perfected down to the last line and gesture. Their mother, for whom the appearance of children had been as much a surprise as if they'd been left on the doorstep by a stork, relied so much on Hester that by the time they grew out of biddable childhood and into their teens (though it was true that Clare remained hardly more than a biddable child), it was Hester they thought of as home. With what remained of their family abroad or indifferent they orbited about her, departing for periods but never quite escaping her pull, so that to retreat to her when all seemed dark and cheerless was not only natural, but essential. When what she thought of as "the Trouble" came (she could never think of Alex as being ill, preferring instead to conceive of it all as being part of his character, and one for which there was no cure), it was her phone that rang first, and her hands which were needed, so that when harried nurses said, "Your mother's here," no one corrected them, because no one had noticed.

She heard their voices almost at the door—*alone and no one sees me*—and put the glass eye back in its place. Wet from her mouth it looked more alive than ever; she turned off the lights and went down the hall to the kitchen, calling them home.

Friday

All the day that followed John remembered the quiet splash of the young man striking the water, the constant shadow on his bare arm and the scent of algae drying on the rocks. The hour spent by the reservoir became part of the fabric of the house and its history; it had the effect of weighting him there. The next morning he'd have been startled and offended if anyone had stopped him at the door to his room and said, "But what on earth are *you* doing here?"

At breakfast Alex said nothing to his sister, nor to Hester as she stood frying eggs in spitting oil and stacking them on a tin plate. But passing John a mug of dark brown tea, he'd given him first a wink, and then a slow-growing smile of such frank happiness that Eve paused on the threshold and said, "Well now. And what are you boys planning?"

"We're going swimming today," said Clare. She had plaited her hair into two untidy ropes that fell over her shoulders. The effect should have been childlike, but it bared her unflawed face and pale mouth, and she looked more like a tomb carving than ever. The cat dragged a fried egg over to where she sat, and crouched between her outstretched arms lapping at the yolk. "Can we? You said today we could go swimming."

"My darling, we've said so every morning since the end of spring." Eve, wearing a shirt that smelled a little of Walker's cigarettes, sat beside John and drew up her legs. The long fine bones of her shins gleamed in the light.

"No—everybody's going, they said they would. Walker said so, and John."

"John?" Eve drew out his name across several low notes, and her eyes glittered as she surveyed him through steam rising from the cup she cradled loosely between her palms. He shifted in his seat, feeling the insistent rasp of the other man's jeans. They were thinning and frayed, and in several places burned with cigarettes, and he'd found in its pockets a long steel screw which he lined up, with the others, on the windowsill. He'd chosen a white shirt that morning, but its sleeves were too short and he'd folded them neatly back toward the elbow. He found the sight of his own bare arm peculiarly unsettling, noticing for the first time how the dark hairs clustered at the bones of his wrists. The shirt was missing its top button, and John felt the woman's gaze pass, amused, over his bare throat. "Our John, out swimming?" The black arch of her eyebrow plainly doubted it; then she lost her brief interest in him and wandered out to the garden, leaving John once again feeling that she found him foolish.

"Well, anyway—I'm not going in first," said Clare. "Will it be cold?" She was wearing a child's swimming costume worn to gray netting at the seams. It was far too small, and left red welts on her shoulders. The promise of a swim had woken her early—John had heard someone light-footed run past his door not long after sunrise, slamming doors in the kitchen downstairs and throwing windows open.

"That depends on when you go in," said John, remembering his nephews once dragging him toward an incoming tide. "Wait till after lunch, and the water will be warm as a bath and you'll forget you ever stood on dry land."

She nodded and said, "All right then," and scooping the cat under her arm followed Eve out into the garden.

"The trouble with my sister," said Alex, turning

away from the sink where he was inexpertly washing up, "is that she does as she's told. You have to watch that."

"I imagine you do," said John.

Late in the morning, on his way to the garden, John found Hester seated on the step where two nights before he'd answered the phone. She was sewing buttons onto a blue and white striped shirt, which showed patches of dust and grease where she held it, her needle flashing in the light coming through the panes in the front door.

"John," she'd said when she saw him, not looking up from her work, "is all as it should be, out there in the sun?" Crouched there with her back pressed against the wooden stairs she looked childish and ancient all at once, and was placed at the center of things. Her gaze took in the blue dining room and the kitchen, and—if she leaned against the banister—along the hall to the door leading out to the garden. Little could happen that would not be seen or heard.

"Elijah's asleep in the dining room with the cat on his shoulder, and Walker's dead-heading the roses. Clare says she won't go swimming after all—she's afraid she'll cut her feet on the stones."

She nodded twice, and then once more after a pause,

as though she had given a problem some thought and reached a conclusion. She broke a length of cotton in her teeth, and sucked at the end to draw it through her needle. "And Alex?"

"I saw him sleeping in the long grass."

She nodded again, without surprise, and looked up from her mending to give him one of her sudden transforming smiles. It was impossible not to smile in return, and John stood watching the needle slip through the button and the fabric in a deft practiced rhythm. Then she said, "*You'll* look after them for me, won't you, dear John?" and this time mischief tugged at her smile, so that he felt irresistibly drawn into a conspiracy.

"I'm going outside now," he said, "to brave the sun." The needle flashed through the cloth, and he imagined she was sewing not a faded shirt, but a fine net that drew them all together. As he put his hand to the door, she called after him: "When you see Alex, will you tell him I found the book he asked me for, and left it in the dining room, where he always sits?"

When he found Alex on the terrace picking moss from the lead face of the sundial, he passed on the message word for word with the accuracy of a clever schoolboy. The younger man frowned, scratching at an insect bite at the rim of the shadow-mark on his arm. "A book?" He shook his head. "But I don't remember any . . ." Then he shrugged. "Oh well—so often I forget what I've done and said, and if I didn't have Hester to remind me . . ." He grinned ruefully, and patting John's shoulder in thanks stepped through the glass doors and into the dining room behind.

Later still Clare came and sat beside him in the long shadow of the dying elm. She'd covered her swimming costume with a dark green dress that reached to her ankles, its hem splashed with mud from another season. Sweat had darkened the roots of her hair, and she was smeared with cream that lay on her skin like the marks on an animal's pelt. The lotion smelled a little of honey, and had begun to attract tiny black flies. "Thunderbugs," said John, lifting one from the back of her hand with his thumbnail. "It means the storm's coming soon."

"I don't think I want to go swimming," she said. The cat had broken the string of beads, and she tossed them between her hands.

"Why—aren't you hot? Won't the water cool you?" He picked up a bead from where it had fallen, and put it in her palm.

"I went up there just now and there was something under the water, like hair or clothes. Alex says it's a plastic bag but a plastic bag would float, wouldn't it?"

"Aren't you going to the seaside tomorrow? Then you can swim in the sea."

"That would be even deeper, though. Do you like swimming?"

"I don't know," he said again. "I can't remember." This was true—there must have been swimming, he thought, on those short bed-and-breakfast holidays in Suffolk and Kent, but he was too dazed with heat to remember. He felt sweat collect where the girl's shoulder rested against his, and moving away from her lowered himself onto the grass. She spread the beads in her lap and began to sort them, chatting idly to him without pausing for breath or answer.

Her undemanding presence soothed him until he lay half-asleep, now and then caught by a word or phrase: "The beads are pretty, aren't they, blue like bits of a broken plate—are they glass? . . . I tried to make him wear them but he wouldn't—he said they smelled like the skin of the dead man who'd been wearing them but I can't smell anything, can you? . . . I remember someone at St. Jude's had beads just like this on her wrist with a bird hanging from it and when she lost the bird I found it for her . . . oh yes, it's hot but we mustn't complain Hester says; it wasn't like this last year when it rained and rained and Eve was unhappy then and wouldn't play the piano, and the keys got dusty . . .

well, of course that was before Walker got here but I don't know why that would cheer her up; she's always hated him and I heard him call her bitch once when he thought no one was listening. *Bitch*, I said, *that's terrible, you can't say that!* and he laughed and said, *Well, she's more like a cat really, a dog's a faithful thing*, and kissed me on the forehead like he always does when he's sorry . . . and of course that was the year we took Alex away . . ."

At this she fell silent, so that the sound of the beads clicking in her lap roused John, who looked up between outspread fingers to see her frowning over her shoulder, back toward the house. After a while she began singing under her breath: *Oh, thunderbug fly away home, your house is on fire and your children will burn . . .* The low hum went through her and into the hard earth, and became part of the heat and the dry rustle of wind in the dying branches of the elm. Soon after he must have fallen asleep, because when he was woken by Clare shaking him urgently by the shoulder it had begun to grow dark, and the empty garden was in shadow.

The sound of a dog barking frantically reached them from the open windows of the house, and with it an unfamiliar voice raised in hysterical anger or pleading. John sat up too quickly, and felt the blood drain from his head. Specks of light floated in front of his eyes;

shaking his head to be rid of them, he asked the girl, "What's that, who's come here? Who is it?" His first thought was that he'd been finally found out, and his stomach lurched once and then receded, leaving him breathless and hollow.

Clare twisted the fabric of her skirt. "I think it's that woman again . . ."

"What woman?"

"She never told us her name . . . She comes sometimes, because—" She stopped herself, pressing her hand to her mouth as if she'd suddenly remembered there were things she mustn't say. Then she slid her hand into his and said, "You won't let her come down here?"

"Of course I won't," he said, thinking of the name written in the notebook upstairs, and engraved into the table in the kitchen. Was this Eadwacer then, come to deliver another of those foolish letters?

"Let's stay here." Clare crouched beside him clasping her knees, and whispered: "She always goes away after a while, let's just stay here where she won't see us—where's Alex? She mustn't find him." Up on the embankment wall, John could see the young man pacing back and forth. The yellow light above the tower had come on, and shed a sickly glow on the grass. "It's all right, he's up there," he said. "Who is she?"

"She's horrible—she shouts and cries, and always brings her dog. And I don't like looking at her face—it's all soft, like she doesn't have any bones. Alex knew her, you know, back when he went away. She's always trying to find him." She started to cry, and John patted her helplessly on the shoulder.

Then there was a lull in the noise from the house, and instead they heard Elijah's deep and measured voice. The dog barked once more, in a single threatened yelp, and the cat bolted from the house with its ragged ears flattened against its scalp. Spying John and Clare huddled at the foot of the elm, it slowed to a saunter, and reaching them thrust its head into Clare's palm and set up an ecstatic purr. The girl fussed over it for a while, and then said, "I can see her, look."

As it grew darker, the lamplit rooms of the house became more distinct, and they could make out a small group in the kitchen, stiffly ranged against each other. Hester and Elijah stood side by side, their backs to the window, making a barrier. Elijah spoke, the lights making an untidy halo of the reddish curls on his head, his hand raised in a defensive soothing gesture. In the center of the room John saw a short woman with thick colorless hair and a pale soft face twisted with anger or misery. She wore a shapeless gray coat buttoned to the neck, and light reflecting from the thick lenses of her glasses gave her movements a blind menacing look. The sight of her fractured John's false sense of belonging—it seemed to him that she'd come to spite him, and he felt a surge of loathing and disgust, as though he'd woken up to find a spider on his pillow. Eve and Walker stood in the doorway, Eve a little behind the older man as though he'd pushed himself forward to shield her. The fine bones of her face were pale as paper underneath her cap of black hair, and her head was tilted back like a child trying to be brave. It was this, and not Clare crying beside him, that made John stand and say, "Do you think we should stay here? Shouldn't we go in?"

She shook her head, and sniffed at her tears. "I don't think so. They always make her go away. Won't you stay with me here until she goes?"

"But don't you think it must be her, who writes those letters? Perhaps she came to put another through the door, and they caught her at it, and there was a scene . . ." The idea satisfied him, as it would if he'd been sitting in his armchair at the shop, idly turning the pages of a book; but all the same there was a nervous twisting of his stomach.

"I don't know. Maybe—but stay here, please. I don't like the shouting, it scares me."

"Of course I will." Her face, streaked with tears and dust, was suddenly very like his brother's had been when he'd come to John with the terrible, brief distress of childhood. He patted her shoulder twice, and said, "Well then, let's not think about her. Why don't you tell me about your cat? How old is he?"

"I don't know." She wiped her nose on her bare arm. "I think he must be very old, look—he has white hairs on his nose." The cat shot John a baleful stare, and began to worry at its torn ear. "Is it true that all ginger cats are boys?"

"Toms, yes. They call them toms, I think—look, is she going?" The little group in the kitchen was slowly dispersing, and he thought he heard the front door close. A moment later the dog's bark receded into the distance, and after a long silence in which they could make out the footsteps of Alex pacing the embankment wall behind them, Eve began to play the piano. The cat, sensing the crisis had passed, aimed a petulant scratch at Clare and idled back toward the house, pausing now and then to pat at something in the grass.

Clare began to cry again, this time quietly and with a steady fixed look of sadness. She seemed to John less like a child then than she'd ever been, and it made him anxious and unsure of himself and his methods; he took his arm from her shoulder and said, "Let's bring your brother in, shall we? Look, here he comes—don't let him see you cry." She reached up her arms, and he pulled her to her feet. "That's right, everything's all right," he said, patting his pockets for the handkerchief that was always there, forgetting he wore another man's clothes. "It's just us now, there's no one else here."

Saturday

I

With the bright sea at his feet and at his back a black rock, John sat listening on the shore:

"... warm in the water like a bath, it's so shallow—Hester, *do* go in ..."

"Look, what's this one then, all spotty like an egg; what is it, Eve, did you see one like it before?"

"... a cowrie, I think—and if I don't play *at all* today I won't be able to do any *at all* tomorrow—my fingers will hurt and be stiff ..."

"I shall *not* go in, however warm, however shallow. A cowrie, yes—how many have you there? They're fortune-teller's shells, if you know how to use them."

"... three ... four ... five ... once I caught a shell

alive . . . Walker give me that one there, there, *there* by your foot . . ."

"John asleep again, I see. What have you done with my cigarettes?"

". . . a necklace of them like this, maybe a starfish in the middle . . ."

"A *whole day* without music. What a waste."

"Where else but where you put them—shall we eat? I'm hungry and the bread is still warm . . . sing, then Eve, if you must, there was singing before anything else . . . No, don't wake him, don't be unkind!"

". . . don't feel like singing, my head aches. Oh, blow it the other way, can't you . . ."

"It'll keep away flies."

". . . and besides, what have you done with Alex?"

"Yes, where's my brother? I want to show him these: thirteen . . . fourteen . . ."

"I recall a poem once in my youth, in those days when we memorized them and they lodged in there— *the opal and the sapphire of that wandering western sea,* it went—I don't recall the rest—and at that time I had an opal ring and honestly thought, *honestly thought,* look hard enough, Hester, and you'll see the white waves moving . . ."

"Remember we used to keep the shells that were still on their hinges and you'd try and keep pennies inside? Sing for us, Evie, go on . . . oh, look, where have you been—I've been waiting and waiting! Look what I found!"

"*No doubt did you please you could marry with ease . . .*"

". . . still warm, thank you—and is there cheese?"

"*When young maidens are fair many lovers will come . . .*"

"But you're not fair, my darling, are you? Clare, now, she's fair as the moon . . ."

"And no maiden either!"

"*But she whom you wed should be North Country bred . . .* give me the knife."

". . . fair little sister, never growed up—show me your treasures then . . ."

"I had thought Elijah might join us this time, really I did, but his times are in his own hands, I daresay—oh, careful now, mind John . . ."

And John, sand kicked into his eyes and the shade retreating from his feet, sat up, took the bread that was offered to him, and said, "It was always a favorite song of my mother's, that one, though I don't think she'd ever been north."

After they'd eaten, and all but Hester had wandered out toward the long shallow pool that lay between them and the sea, John said: "I think I'll go for a walk." Hester waved something between a farewell and a blessing, and resumed her watchful cross-legged position on the red blanket.

He'd woken that morning resolved to take his leave—the notebook left for the other man, the letter folded twice, the painted Puritan saluted at the door—but somewhere along the way he'd been caught up again, helpless, Elijah waving them farewell at the door, and delivering (or so John thought) a slow complicit wink. Still sleepy when they set out, he dozed fitfully in the moist hot air of the car, so that he only recalled waking now and then to see rabbits poisoned by farmers shivering at the roadside, and pylons coming at him across the fields like high-masted ships of the line. Stumbling to his feet, he'd seen a parking lot sloping to a quayside, where a boy sat cross-legged trailing a crab line in green water. There was the familiar scent of clean air and salt and something deeper underneath, of fragments of fish dropped by gulls and drying out in hidden places, and seaweed dying on beds of rock; and above the calling of the gulls, the rushing and receding he'd once taken home in the coils of a shell that he pressed to his ear in winter, when there seemed no possibility of the sun ever shining again.

Returning now to the parking lot, uncertain of his way, he looked out to the line of dark squat shrubs that marked the beginning of the salt marsh. The child had abandoned his fishing lines and now leaned against the hull of a blue-painted tender, scratching patterns on the tarmac with a piece of flint.

The marshes were reached from a narrow raised pathway along a bank that formed a kind of sea wall. As John set out on the path he paused to let a toad cross; it splayed out its soft patient feet and crept past, a pulse throbbing in its stomach and its butter-colored eyes rolling thanks. To his right as he walked were the long narrow gardens of the last houses before the sea; to his left, several feet below, was the low stretch of land that was drowned and revived every day by the industrious tides. It was an indistinct landscape riddled with irregular channels that ran into and out of each other everywhere he looked. Late in the day water would seep from under the soft mud and trickle unhurriedly in fine rivulets, gathering speed until the tide was high.

The land through which these channels ran was piebald green and blue, covered in grasses and fat blades of samphire or broad patches of sea lavender, its flowers so fine it might have been a bluish mist settling at ankle height, rolling in from the sea. It was impossible to believe it could ever have been underwater, but here and there a fine dark lacework of seaweed lay on the tips of the grasses, hanging like cobwebs in a forgotten room.

It was not a wholly unfamiliar scene—his brother had taken him to places like it often over the years. "These salt flats are an eerie sort of place," Christopher had written to him, soon after he moved to the coast: "You couldn't possibly stand alone out there under that massive sky and not feel *something*." On his first visit John had seen how empty it was, and how doleful, and felt nothing but the damp chill of a winter morning. That a man's spirit could be brought low by nothing more than empty sky over empty land was absurd, he'd thought, and thumped his brother's shoulder with cheerful force as they walked home.

He came down from the raised shingle track onto a broad stretch of cracked mud on which white salt stains glittered. Above him the sky was bright and the small hard sun pricked at his scalp. From away to his left, deep in a channel he couldn't see, a curlew began to sing with a bubbling call that might have come from underwater.

He stooped to pick a head or two of sea lavender,

wincing as the sturdy sharp stems rasped against the flesh in the crook of his fingers. The flowers were papery and dry, and held no scent. "All will be well," said John hopelessly to a herring gull dozing on a wooden boat nearby. "All will be well, and all manner of things will be well." It was plain the gull doubted this, and with a tired thrust of its wings it abandoned its wooden perch. John, who hadn't noticed the boat when first coming down from the embankment path, walked curiously over. By far the largest of the crafts stranded on the marshes, it was an ugly, ill-proportioned, unpainted thing, with no rudder, mast or sail that he could see, as unseaworthy as a garden shed. A black stovepipe stuck up from the roof of the cabin, reaching down to a grimed oven that could just be seen through the center of the boat's three windows.

Moving a little closer, setting his feet carefully on the few raised firm patches between the damp rivulets of mud, John peered in. The window on the left was half open, and swayed now and then in the breeze, sending the reflected sun sliding back and forth over the smeared glass. Three pans, untidily stacked, sat on the stovetop; a clean towel hung on a wooden rail. On a shelf nailed over the stove was a tin can with its bright label turned to the wall, and a childish egg cup with a blue stripe. If he stood on tiptoe it was possible to see, in the center of a pine table pushed under the window, a stack of blue napkins ironed into neat squares, and a magazine with half its cover in shade, and half bleached pale by the sun. The boat was stranded in a stretch of damp mud as pale as the cap of a mushroom—no one could possibly reach it from the soft wet marshes without floundering. A set of tracks, plainly showing the paws of a curious dog, led halfway to the tilting hull and back again at the anxious call of its master. Where the drier marshes met the mud several wooden planks were stacked, caked with mud and in places draped with seaweed. They made a dry path out to the boat a short distance away, but there were no marks in the mud. John watched it a while, half-expecting to see a face at the window, but there was only his own, thinner than he remembered it, and anxious under an untidy thatch of hair.

Turning away, he returned to the path and followed it toward the empty horizon. Small furtive movements came from the grasses and sea lavender at his ankles, and sometimes a gull screamed out. Behind the stranded houseboat, beyond the embankment path, a line of pine trees showed black against the empty sky. Pigeons squabbled in the branches, bursting out of one tree and furiously into another. John watched them, peering through the black thicket. The sun raged at him—he felt it burning through the thin weave of his shirt and sending the blood to his head, where it beat implacably behind his eyes. A woman and child coming down the shingled path looked at him, startled, as they passed, the woman tugging at the boy's hand to walk a little distance away from him. She had a pleasant soft face tanned by a week's holiday; the boy was small, thin-legged, inquisitive, his green T-shirt still damp at the edges from the sea. Not sharing his mother's suspicion, he eyed John frankly as he passed, taking him in with the same joyful interest he showed in the deep-cut channel and the listing boats.

"Look, look," he said, seeing the window on the houseboat swing open and shut. "Is someone in there? Can we see? Do they live inside?"

"I don't think so. It's too old. No one lives there now."

The two stood side by side at the edge of the pool of mud, dampened by thin channels of rising water. "Yes they do, they do—look." The boy jumped up and down to see better. "They've had their dinner, look." The woman peered in. "A long time ago, maybe. There's no one there now."

"But I want to go inside!" His voice rose with indignation.

"Well. You can't."

"Why not?"

"Why do you think?"

John had almost reached the path. Beside the wooden houseboat, the boy tugged thoughtfully at his T-shirt. "Because it isn't mine?"

"That's right. It's not ours, so we can't go in." The woman smoothed his hair, then said: "Listen! Can you hear that funny sound again?" She stooped to crouch beside the boy and turning him toward her put her head beside his. "Be quiet, and listen, there it is again!"

The child cupped his hands behind his ears and pulled them comically forward, straining into the breeze. John heard it too: the mournful bubbling call not far away now, hidden somewhere in the marsh. "It's a curlew," he said, not quite to himself. The boy heard him and turned sharply.

"That man said something!" he whispered loudly, looking at John with astonishment. The woman stood and turned to John, her eyebrows raised.

"It's a curlew," he said again apologetically. "You can tell because he sounds like he's singing under the sea. Like there are bubbles coming out of his beak." He smiled at the boy. "Listen. Can you hear it?" There was nothing for a while, then it came again, starting on a high fluting note and falling unevenly through a scale. "You'll know it when you see it," said John, "because his beak turns down at the end, like this." He made a curving gesture, and the child glanced quickly at his mother—could this be true?—and back, wide-eyed, at John. "Watch out for it," he said. "It won't fly very high. It's just a brown old thing, really. Quite ordinary. You wouldn't notice it, in a crowd." He smiled at them both and turned back to the path.

"Thank you," said the woman, smiling uncertainly at him. Then she said, "Say thank you!" and the boy did, twisting the green fabric of his T-shirt around a dirty thumb.

When John was only a few feet along the embankment path he heard the call again, and the young child shouting. *They've seen it*, he thought, and hoped they'd not be disappointed.

Late in the afternoon he found Hester sitting alone with her back to the rock, her hands clasped over her stomach. "You've been gone a long time. I was worried—it would be easy to get lost, out there. I did once." She gave the impression she'd done so only out of choice, and enjoyed every minute of it.

"I heard curlews singing, and the tide coming in— look: I picked some sea lavender." He'd tied the bunch with a ribbon of grass, and blushed when he gave it to her.

"John! How sweet you are, and the flowers won't fade, you know—there are bunches in the greenhouse someone must have picked just when the last century turned. Sit down, won't you, and have a drink with me— let's see if it's kept cold, all tombed up in the sand . . ." John took a bottle of beer from her and sank into the meager shade. There was no sign of the rising tide— the sea was as far away as ever, and hadn't yet reached the long pool which was busy with children, and with old women who'd wet their feet and would go no farther.

"You're all alone here, then?" He fell to wondering where Eve might have gone, and whether she'd kept the sun from scorching her skin. He thought of the curlew's call, and wished she'd heard it too.

"Clare's over there"—Hester jerked her head to the left, where he could see the girl stooping to the sand, her amber hair falling over her eyes—"collecting shells. She's making a picture in the sand—a tree, I think—it's not very good." She paused, scratched her head, and seemed about to speak, but changed her mind. "Alex has been swimming but he's there now, can you see? He seems to have made a new friend." Not far away, between their disarrayed blankets and books and the shallow pool, Alex crouched and spoke to a child. Leaning forward John saw the green T-shirt and recognized the inquisitive boy from an hour or so before. "Oh yes,

I spoke to him earlier on the marshes—his mother can't be far away."

"Children adore Alex—they climb all over him like he's a friendly dog." She watched the two with such pride and gentleness, it transformed her face: her fine eyes seemed to broaden and spread, pushing at the lines and furrows that coarsened her features, making her, for a brief moment, handsome as a healthy girl. Catching John's eye, she flushed, and the effect fractured; she looked, he thought, rather astonished, guilty, as if she'd been caught out in a secret vice. "Here comes Clare," she said, rearing up on her knees and waving the bunch of drying sea lavender over her head: "Move along a little, John—the shadows are getting longer now, there's plenty of room."

II

Things have changed—I can feel it from here. My mother used to go out onto the doorstep at the end of summer and scent the air like a dog and say, "Change of season coming," and go back inside and put the kettle on as if she felt a chill. It was always hard to believe she could be right, but it would never be long before the leaves turned. I saw it happen yesterday: not just the end of the heat wave—though thank God, I think it's coming—but one complete and final change, as if the tide's going out and won't ever come back again.

In the house where I grew up, there was a painting in the dining room. I always took the same seat at the table (even now I'll sit with my back to the window and with the wall to my right, if I can—anything else makes me uneasy), and I could see it as I ate. Years later I found a copy and meant to hang it in the shop, although I never did. The picture shows a woman in a black dress with a pale anxious face, sitting at a dinner table. You can just see a man sitting almost out of the frame, and he's talking to her, but she isn't listening—she's looking straight out of the canvas. She has a small mouth, and it's half open, as if she's waiting for someone and has just seen them coming. She has a glass of red wine in her hands, and on the table in front of her there's a jug of wine so dark it looks black. There are lamps with red shades, and the flowers on the table are red, and red catches the silver candlesticks and the ice bucket on the white tablecloth. The whole painting is saturated with color and light, and seeing it there was like finding a gap in the drab walls of the house, with something realer and more vivid just on the other side. When I was young it used to frighten me—I didn't think a painting should look at me like that. Sometimes I'd stand directly in front of it, and see my own reflected face laid over hers, and I would wonder which of us was painted, and who was watching whom.

Everything that happened today brought that painting back to me as clearly as if it were hanging on the wall between the windows. I've been outside them all looking in, or thought I had; it has been as though I were holding them in my hands between the covers of a book, so that when I grow tired of them I can set them all down and find a better story elsewhere. But I begin to feel myself being drawn against my will—it's as if one day I passed that painting and from the corner of my eye saw the woman in the black dress reaching out to give me a glass of wine.

After I came back from walking on the salt marsh I sat with Hester for a long time. The day I saw her first she'd looked at me as if I'd been numbers scribbled on a piece of paper that could be added up, and I felt as if she knew me then as well as anyone ever has, or is likely to. I wish I hadn't described her as ugly. I've seen what happens to that face of hers when she looks at Alex— her bright dark eyes seem to refine and illuminate the rest of her, and make her beautiful.

We sat together watching the emptying beach. I could see the child I'd spoken to, playing with Alex in the shallow pool between the rocks and the sea—I remembered wondering where his mother had gone, but by then it was late in the afternoon and I was tired, and my head had begun to ache. The pieces of rock where we sat soaked up the sun, and sent its heat into my blood and bones. Every time I opened my eyes I'd see Hester still sitting like Buddha with her legs crossed, patiently watching Alex playing with the child, and each time the tall boy with his hair lit amber by the sun and the child in his green T-shirt would be farther away until we couldn't hear them laughing and shrieking in the water anymore. When I closed my eyes for the last time it must have been to sleep for a long while, because I was woken by the sound of footsteps thudding into the sand. At first I thought it was my own blood beating in my head but it grew nearer and louder, and when I looked up a woman was running toward us with her arms outspread, shouting. When she reached us she kicked up the sand and it went in my eyes, and for a moment I was blinded. I turned away and cleared them, and recognized her as the woman I'd last seen on the marshes, telling her son to thank the strange man who'd known the sound of a curlew.

She'd been crying, and must have come a long way—sweat dripped from her forehead into her eyes and ran down with the tears and gathered into a stream under her chin. "Have you seen him?" she was saying. "My boy—he's in a green T-shirt—have you seen him? I've been looking and I can't find him. He was with a man with red hair—did you see him?" All of this came out between deep rasping breaths, and her eyes were so wide I could see the whites of them all around. I tried to get up but my legs had gone to sleep, and I had to brace myself against the rock. Hester took her by the shoulders and said, "Calm down, sweetheart, calm down, stop and breathe. That's right, we'll find him, he won't be far. That's right; that's right." She said those last words over and over until it was really just a soft and soothing hiss: *'ssri, 'ssri* . . . Then the woman recognized me, and turned her body slightly to catch me in her distress. I felt it reach me—the pulse in my head began to beat harder and faster. The woman's anguish was horrible— although she was calmer she shivered violently, and the skin was drawn tight across her cheekbones, making her seem to have been starved in the short space since I'd seen her last. Hester remained as she always was, a solid calm presence, still murmuring to the woman so that she too had to lower her voice, although she asked the same question over and over—"Have you seen him? Where's he gone? Did you see him? Where's he gone?"

Hester questioned her, as if she had authority over her and the whole beach and everyone on it: the poor woman had fallen asleep, beaten into the shade by the sun and worn out by the wind. She'd watched her son from the corner of her eye as he played with a kind young man on a half-empty beach where surely no one was ever lost or hurt. He was a talkative boy and trusting, but not stupid; sure he'd talk to strangers but not go anywhere with them; he knew better than that. She berated herself for having fallen asleep—"But he seemed so nice, just a young man, not much more than a boy himself really; they were just over there and I was so tired . . ." While she was still talking, pleading partly for help and partly for forgiveness, Hester—still gripping the woman's hands—turned to me and said, very calmly and quietly, "Can you see Alex?"

My eyes were still sore from the sand and my vision was blurred, but I shaded them from the sun and scanned the beach back and forth two or three times. The light coming back from the hard-packed white sand was so dazzling I felt it pierce through to my already aching head, and it was hard to tell what was heat haze pooling on the beach, and where the sea began. I could see Clare crouching by her collected shells nearby, making spirals out of cockle shells and not noticing the tension that had suddenly bound us tightly to a stranger. Our three shadows reached her red plastic bucket and made it dark, but she didn't look up. Farther off a tall pair made thin and fragile by the distance walked slowly at the water's edge. "I can't see him." I said. "I don't think he's there." My words went further and did more than I meant them to. The woman had given in to Hester's soothing, but when she heard me she stiffened, became combative. "That man he was with, the young man with the red hair, he's with you?"

"He's with me," said Hester.

The other woman had been holding Hester's hands, or letting her own be held, but when she heard this she pulled them out, and her eyes, which hadn't left the other woman's face, narrowed with sudden distrust. I felt the air change slightly as her anxiety flared into anger. She'd been angry before, but it had been turned inward and made into guilt. What I'd said gave her liberty to fling it at other targets. Hester stepped away from her and held up her hands like someone fending off a blow. The woman said, "What . . ." and shook her head violently. "What? He's with you? Then . . ." Stumbling on the sand, which must have burned her bare feet, she moved quickly round the blankets and books and empty water bottles that staked our claim to the beach. "Ben?" She pushed past me, not maliciously but because she couldn't really see either of us anymore. "Ben, are you here, can you hear me?" She slid behind the black rocks we'd been leaning against and raised her voice. It was compressed by the rocks and I thought: He wouldn't hear you, even if he was nearby, even if we were keeping him out of sight. "Answer me, darling. Mummy isn't cross with you. Ben? Can you hear me?"

I saw Hester standing with her hands on her hips watching the woman. She was less impassive now, biting hard on her bottom lip. I said, "I saw them together earlier. The boy wanted to see inside one of the boats on the marshes—maybe Alex took him there?" Hester took this in on a low breath, then said, "Right," and gripped my shoulder. She shook her hair back from her forehead. "Look, be quiet—she's coming back." Then she called out: "Sweetheart?" It was an endearment she used without discrimination, but now it had changed; it wasn't mollifying but condescending, as if she could use it to put an opponent in her place. The woman had appeared again from between the rocks; her flash of anger had gone, and she was wringing her hands. "He isn't there, he's not there . . ."

"Of course not"—Hester put an arm across the woman's shoulders—"of course not. We'd've seen him, wouldn't we?" Turning the woman to face her, she put a hand on either side of her face and said intently, "The man he was with is called Alex. Did you speak to him?"

The woman nodded eagerly—her mistrust of Hester had gone, dissolved by the stronger woman's gaze, and she was looking at her again with a desperate pleading face: "Just a bit, an hour ago I think. Ben wanted someone to play football with and my head ached, and the man was nearby—he was young and he smiled at me . . . they were there, just over there"—she flung out her arm—"I don't understand, how could they get so far?" Her voice ended on a drawn-out wail.

"You mustn't panic. You won't find him by crying, now will you?" Hester bent awkwardly and picked up a half-empty bottle of water. "Have some of this." The woman winced as she drank and I thought it would be warm and unpleasant by now. I began to feel agitated by what I knew—the boy had probably begged to be taken back to the boat to spy for faces at the windows, and Alex would have taken him, I was sure of it, not seeing anything to threaten the happy day. I stepped forward and put out my hand thinking I'd tell the woman, but the order of the house had established itself here too, and I deferred to Hester, and stepped back again. Hester waited for the other woman to stop sipping at the bottle, then said, "You were out on the marshes, earlier in the day?" She nodded. "Do you think your son might have gone back there?"

"Not alone. He's only five years old—he would never get that far alone, he'd get lost, he would never go by himself . . ." Then the realization of what she'd said struck her—he wasn't alone and lost, he'd been taken away from her—and she threw down the water bottle. It landed beside Clare, on her knees beside a mandala of cowries. She noticed for the first time the three of us standing there and came over, frowning, looking from me to Hester and back again. She came and stood close by me, smelling of salt. I said, "She's lost her little boy," and she grimaced.

"But we'll find him, John. Won't we?" Then she said to the woman, more loudly, "We'll find him for you," but the woman wasn't listening. Without turning to speak to Hester she ran heavily over the sand and I watched her heels sinking into the fine powder. We three looked at each other and followed, Hester moving a little behind me, and Clare running lightly ahead. I remember watching the woman's bare feet thudding on the concrete of the parking lot and wincing as if I could feel it too, but she went on running and calling her son's name, although even if he'd been able to hear her it came out so high and frantic it was like the seagulls crying. Many of the cars were gone by then, as people had tired of being battered by the sun and had gone home to lie in the shade until evening made life bearable. I looked for the boy with his fishing lines but he was gone too, with his white marks like a threat on the tarmac, and the shed selling crabs and cockles had closed its shutters. I remember being surprised that Hester, carrying so much weight on her stomach and thighs, could run so far and so fast. I could hear her breath heaving in and out of her but it didn't slow her pace, and she reached the edges of the marsh just after us.

By then the tide was coming in fast: fingers of water crept across the cracked mud, and though the woman called and called, and Hester's breath behind me hissed on the back of my neck, I thought I could hear it trickling up from underneath. Then suddenly I couldn't hear anything because the woman stopped in her tracks and put her hands up to her head and screamed, not a high woman's noise but deep and rasping and terrible, and it silenced everything else. I'd never heard anything like it and hope never to again—it dried my tongue and my stomach fell through me. I'd stopped running when I heard it, and Hester ran into me and knocked the breath out of me: I bent double and when I straightened up the woman was silent, which was worse than the screaming, because everything else was silent too, and there was a long empty moment when the water stopped creeping toward us over the mud, and we tried to see what she'd seen. She stood pinned to the ground, her hands still raised to her head, and I thought stupidly that if the wind blew she'd fall where she stood like a toppled statue.

When we moved to either side of her on the narrow path and saw what was coming, Hester gasped and I heard a groan that can't have been from Clare, so I suppose it must have come from me. Coming slowly toward us and with his head bowed and loose so that it swayed a little as he walked was Alex, and he was carrying the child. The bright green T-shirt was muddy and dragged up over his chest. His body sagged between Alex's arms, and one of his sneakers was missing. Alex must have been able to see us on the path but he didn't lift up his head or call out, only went on walking, and the boy's dangling limbs swung as he walked.

I marveled at how slowly and painfully the blood thudded against my ears, and then the woman drew her breath in a gulp and screamed her son's name. She dashed forward, pushing Hester into the rough grass, and snatching the boy, lowered him onto the path. By the time we reached her the child was trying to sit up, and seemed not frightened but dazed. Where the T-shirt was pulled up over his thin torso he had a long fresh graze, and before his mother wrapped him in the cardigan she'd been wearing I saw a few dark splinters in the skin. The woman had become very calm, no more distressed than if her child had caught a cold—she stroked his hair and murmured, "We'd better get you in the warm, hadn't we," although the sun was still trying to scald the water on the marshes. There was a bruise on the child's forehead so recent it was still swelling as I watched, and when I saw it I became aware that Alex was standing a few paces away, wringing his hands and saying, "I'm sorry, I'm so sorry," over and over. His T-shirt, white when we'd left the house that morning, was covered in patches of mud that were like inkblots, making a pattern like the drab wings of a giant moth. He too was grazed, down the length of his right arm.

Clare stood behind me and touched my arm briefly and uncertainly every few moments, as if she wanted to ask me something but couldn't think what it was. I felt we were all ranged against Alex, that battle lines had been scored in the mud on the path: I wanted to place myself exactly halfway between the mother and the man who'd taken her son away, but couldn't move, and as I write it now I feel it was cowardice that made me just stand by. "I'm so sorry," he kept on saying, and I wanted to shout that he should either say nothing at all, or tell us what had happened—what use was "sorry" if he'd done nothing wrong?

The boy was sitting up by then—the cut on his forehead hadn't after all gone deeper than the skin, and there was color in his cheeks. He looked around, seeming unsurprised, not registering Alex's face as any different from all the others that leaned over him. He recognized me. "We heard that funny bird again," he said brightly, and then began to cry. It seemed to me such a simple sound, so straightforward and easily remedied in all the muddle I'd been living through, that it calmed my anxiety, but the effect on the crouching woman was terrible. She stood up, and left unsupported the child almost toppled backward. Clare, with her unselfconscious helpfulness, knelt next to him and patted his back with the same rough uneven strokes she used on her cat. The woman stepped forward toward Alex, who put out his hands and spread them in a gesture of fear, I think, and also of apology. It would be easy to look at the wringing hands and call it guilt, but that wasn't what I saw then, and I don't see it now, in my memory or as I write it out. He said again, "I'm sorry!" but this time making the words firmer, as if it might forestall the woman who was still coming toward him.

When she reached him, she put out her hand either to strike him or grip his arm, then pulled it back as if the idea of touching him disgusted her, and hissing between clenched teeth she said, "What did you do? Did you hurt my son? What have you done?" Alex tried to speak but it came too slowly, and while he still formed the words on a stammer I'd never heard before, the woman said again, with controlled malice: "Well? Talk, can't you? What's wrong with you—cat got your tongue, is it? Say something, tell me what you did!" She was moving toward him still, a small step with every word, and Alex backed away imperceptibly, holding out his hands to ward off the words and not finding any of his own. His silence infuriated the woman and with angry tears she said: "What have you done? What have you done? What have you done?"

Hester, still standing close to Alex, moved forward a little, and I remember then being puzzled at her face, which briefly showed open hostility to a woman who had every cause for anger. If she was going to say something, to defend Alex, to placate her perhaps, we never heard it, because a thought occurred suddenly to the woman and she stopped, gasped and said, not shouting anymore but falteringly, testing the thought: "Did you—did you touch him?"

Seeing the word now, written plainly and without the awful inflection she gave it, it's impossible to think how we all saw at once how to touch could be worse than to hurt. But it hung in the air like a foul smell; Hester paused in her movement and I felt bile rising in my throat. Alex went white and his eyes widened, and the movement of his hands became frantic, as if he felt the accusation against his face and wanted to bat it away.

Only Clare seemed not to have noticed: she and the boy had found something by the path and were parting the grasses to get a better look and I wondered if it was the toad who'd passed me earlier that day. I wanted Alex to shout "No!" and to shout it clearly and strongly to break through the hysteria I could see darkening the woman's face, but he didn't, only mumbled, "Sorry, I'm sorry, it isn't in there, I can't remember," beating his own forehead with a bunched fist, then sagging slightly against Hester's shoulder. It must have looked like a confession, because the woman rushed at him and struck out, not with the comic flailing I see sometimes on my way home late from work, but with violent precision. She wore a ring with a cheap stone on her right hand and it flashed as her arm swung back; Alex flinched and put up his arm, but she was quick and the blow landed and I heard it loud as a knock on a door. He didn't make any sound, and I remember being proud of him for that. The woman's anger exhausted itself quickly, perhaps because when Alex raised his head again he was bleeding from a split lip. The woman ran to her son, who looked now like any child might who'd been playing in the mud somewhere and fallen. He and Clare had picked long broad blades of grass and were trying to blow them like reeds, but they were the wrong kind and made no sound. The woman bent and yanked the boy's arm to make him stand, and he looked up, baffled at first, then remembered where he'd been, and that his head hurt, and started sniffling.

Standing there holding his hand, she turned to face us. By then I'd crossed the battle line and stood with Alex and Hester, feeling the force of her rage pulling me in with them. She said: "I'm calling the police. I'm going to go and get my phone and call the police—you took my son and hurt him, and everyone will know." The child stopped sniffling and rubbed his eyes and nose on his bare arm. Tears and snot made a path through the mud drying on his skin. "It wasn't his fault," he said weakly, and I heard Alex make a small grateful noise, but the woman didn't hear her son, or didn't listen. She turned away from us and began walking back along the path, and I felt Hester move convulsively next to me and draw in her breath to call her back.

But a few paces away the woman stopped. It must have been only a second or two that she stood unsteady on the path, but I felt the moment stretch out in front of us, giving me time to wonder what had happened or might have happened, what would happen to them all now, what it meant for them and me. Then she spun round and said, in a voice she must've taken great efforts to make chilled and controlled: "I want your names. All of them. And your phone number." She said it again, only tried to make it sound professional, as if she could intimidate us, but the words weren't quite right and I almost smiled, because I was ashamed of everyone and frightened for them all: "I require your contact details immediately please, so this matter can be resolved." I think she must have seen my smile because her eyes narrowed and the chill left her voice and I saw the flush of anger or embarrassment creep back into her cheeks.

The woman had found a pen and a scrap of card in her bag, and thrust it at me with shaking hands. Thinking all the while how absurd this was, I wrote out my name in clear capitals, as if I were humoring an inquisitive child. I wanted to say, "You're mistaken; you must be—I never knew anyone less capable of harming a child." But every time I took a breath to speak I remembered my own guilt in deceiving them all, and the old stammer came back, and I couldn't make the words come. I passed the card to Hester, thinking that surely she would speak in his defense, but instead she paused and looked at me with what I think was gratitude, then wrote Alex's name underneath. She made it complete—ALEXANDER—as if this could distance it from the boy she'd sent to bed the night before with a glass of water for the hot night. Then she wrote her own name, and underneath that her telephone number, folded the card, and walked toward the waiting woman, who held out her hand.

Hester put the card into her open palm and folded the other woman's fingers over it, and I heard her say: "I am so sorry your child was hurt. And I am sorry your day is spoiled. But it was an accident, no one touched him. You're making a terrible mistake—and I understand, I do, the world these days is dangerous for children. But it is a mistake. Look at Alexander, look—can't you see he's hurt most of all, that this will take longer to heal than bruises? Call us, call the police, talk to the boy: we're not afraid. We'll talk to you, to anyone. But take him home. Talk to him: he'll tell you."

We watched and waited for an angry response but none came. Hester's strength of will gives her words weight: there's something in her face, although it's ugly—or even perhaps because it's ugly—that seems incompatible with deceit or half-truths. The other woman briefly touched her son's forehead, then nodded at Hester, and walked away from us. Clare stood by her brother plaiting blades of grass. She'd realized by then what had happened, I think, and was leaning against him slightly, biting down on her lip in concentration or perhaps because she didn't want to cry. Hester came back to us. She put out her hand and touched each of us lightly on the shoulder. "Come on," she said. "Time to go home."

Not much was said or done that night. There were phone calls I only partly overheard, Hester saying little and Alex nothing at all. I was there when Hester told Eve and Walker what had happened, and saw Eve storm at Hester as if it had been her fault: "The woman's an idiot. Who leaves a little child alone on a beach?

She should be glad. She should be glad it was Alex who found him, who looked after him. She deserves to have him taken away. I hope she calls the police. I hope she does . . ." Walker put his hand on the back of her neck with a possessive gesture I hated; she flung it off, and shut herself in the music room. She didn't play the melodies I was hoping for but scales, painfully slow and even, and after a while it was like the noise of the crickets in the garden and we couldn't hear it anymore.

I found Elijah in the dining room, dozing in the high-backed chair with its wooden candlesticks, where I'd seen him the night I arrived. His grave quiet presence was a relief to me, and we played chess until Hester came in to draw the curtains against the moths drawn to the light. When I told him what had happened he listened without anger or surprise—either the thought of Alex doing harm was so absurd it deflected off him without sinking in, or he could accommodate the idea of wrongdoing more calmly than we, as being just another consequence of being human. When I finished the miserable tale he shook his head and picked up a white bishop. "I'm afraid I never was any good at chess. You've won again, haven't you?"

Just before I came upstairs to bed I went into the kitchen. Hester was there, unpacking the plastic cups and plates we'd taken to the beach. Clare was there too, knocking the sand from her shoes onto the kitchen floor and being scolded for it; and I didn't notice for a long time that Alex was sitting in one of the kitchen's dark recesses with his legs crossed, inspecting his hands and looking up sometimes when he heard his name.

"She called, of course," Hester told me. She pulled a foil-wrapped parcel from one of the bags. "That's the fruitcake I made, and we never got to eat it," she said, turning it in her hands. It gave off a sickly scent of spice and honey. "Yes—she called, firstly to ask lots of questions. She took the boy to hospital—he'd been knocked out but not for long, though they're keeping him in until tomorrow. Alex spoke to her. She wanted to know if Alex would tell her what the boy had told her. Whether it all added up."

"And it did," Clare told me.

"Well, of course it did. The boy had lied to Alex. He told him his mother had gone to the marshes to look at the boats, and he was scared to go out and meet her on his own, and would Alex take him. There's no one on earth who can lie as well as a child, because they believe themselves, so it comes out like the truth." She gave me another of her searching looks and I wondered what Elijah had told her. But she shrugged and said, "They went out to the marsh and she wasn't there, of course. No one was. And the boy ran off to look at some abandoned boat. He slipped and fell, and if Alex hadn't been there he'd've lain out there on the mud while the tide came in."

I asked her if the woman would carry out her threat to call the police, and she said, "I doubt it. What would she say? That she left her child alone and wasn't there when he fell? That this man saved him and she thanked him with violence?" She nodded at Alex. The wound on his lip was closing but the flesh was swollen and he darted out his tongue to moisten it. "I imagine she's ashamed of herself. She should be."

Hester took a sandy blanket out of the bag and shook it, then folded it against her breast, and as she did she sent one of her long bright looks over to the corner where Alex was sitting. I saw something then that I couldn't believe—something so peculiar that I blinked my eyes to clear them and looked again to be certain of it. Alex had pulled his knees up under his chin, and was pressing himself against the kitchen wall as if he wanted to seep into the bricks and plaster. But Hester didn't look angry that he'd been accused of something so unthinkable, or afraid the woman had seen something in him that had passed the rest of us by. I didn't find in her face the confused pity I was feeling, or even the most straightforward things—tiredness and hunger

and anxiety. What I found instead was a long slow look
of satisfaction, like a woman who'd come to the end of
a day's work sooner than expected. Then she smiled,
and it wasn't the sudden unfeigned smile that comes
when you least expect it, but a kind of smirk.

It shocked me more than anything else that day, and
made everything I'd seen up to that moment shift and
sharpen. I fumbled for a chair and knocked a knife to
the floor. They all turned to stare at me, except Alex,
who scratched over and over at the graze on the back of
his hand. Hester turned very slowly away from him and
said, "All right there, John?" and smiled at me. It was
the same warm, steady gaze that had greeted me when
I arrived, in the same kindly ugly face, and everything
shifted again and settled into its old patterns.

Soon after that I came upstairs, and set it all down.
These words on the page are problems I can't solve,
but I'll keep at it—and sooner or later I'll work them
all out . . .

Sunday

I

It had always been Walker's habit to get up early and steal a march on the day. It had annoyed his mother, braced for a teenage son tangled in his sheets at noon; and it annoyed his wife, who wanted to be alone in the mornings when there was a chance of finding a jay on the lawn. But there it was: he found himself alert the moment his eyes opened; smoked before he drank or ate; and was never seen to be weary. Once—early on, before the days took on their pattern—Hester thought she'd beaten him to the kitchen, and had, laughing, laid out plates with a ringing of china on wood fit to quicken the dead, but he'd appeared a moment later, his gray hair bath damp, smelling a little of cedar and on his second cigarette.

On the morning of John's fifth day, which Elijah

would once have called *the Lord's Day* (and still did, sometimes, when he forgot to mind his language), Walker stood in the greenhouse watching the sun come up. The pitched roof with its lapping glass tiles filtered the early light through a rime of lichen and moss, so that it cast a greenish pall upon the floor. Already the air was thick with moisture, and Walker pushed open a window and watched the reflected garden slide across the pane. He stood a while with his face turned to the opening, feeling a slight chill that would be gone within the hour. The sun had reached the high grass verge that bounded the reservoir, and he wondered where Alex had slept that night, if he'd slept at all—once they'd found him lying at the foot of the embankment, as if he'd climbed from the reservoir, and falling exhausted down the incline slept like a child where he lay.

The events of the day before were so vivid still that Walker wouldn't have been surprised to find the woman at the window with the child in her arms. He hadn't seen her, or the wound on the boy's forehead, but overnight conjured up a lesion that opened to the bone, and eyes upturned to show their whites. Was it possible that Alex had hurt the boy? After all he was not well . . . He stooped to pick up a snail's shell cleaned of its meat, and tossed it from palm to palm. It was weightless, and when he closed his fist it turned almost to dust. No—he could not believe that, or wouldn't, at least. He opened his hand and let the fragments fall to the unswept floor.

Before Walker had come, the greenhouse had been locked for a decade or more. He'd had no interest in it at first, with its sour damp smell of neglect, though he and Eve had idly tried the key one night and found the swollen door could not be moved. It was Elijah who'd finally forced his way in, setting his shoulder to the door and leaving a dent in the rotten wood. Walker had found him that same day in a cane armchair that listed on a broken leg. He'd mislaid the half-frown that gave him a constant grave sad look and smiling said: "It's the nearest I can bear to going outside. I can see the sky—I almost feel the wind!"

Together they'd unwound the lengths of cord that fastened the windows, and flung them open. Stale air crossed the painted wooden windowsills and left behind a very faint scent of peat and even—though only Walker claimed to have smelled it—of pollen and green leaves.

The greenhouse had been built hastily, on a whim, and in high winds the window frames creaked at their joints and shed thick fragments of paint. The floor was paved in terra-cotta, and the bodies of ants clotted in the seams where the tiles were joined. At night it took on the appearance of a small shadowed grove—the remains of vines and roses would seem to bloom in the quarter-light, and it was possible to imagine, above the dust and damp, the shocking scent of jasmine opening at night. In the corner a vase that belonged elsewhere held a bunch of purple sea lavender, its colors bright as the morning it was cut.

Walker, who knew what work could be found for idle hands, took to spending mornings counting out seeds in their paper packets and pinning faded botanical prints to the walls. One morning he found under a bench a cactus in a mossy pot that had survived its long drought. It was grayish, like the skin of someone kept from daylight, and covered in spines that caught in the fabric of his shirt and irritated him later that night. Kneeling on the hard floor, he'd rocked back on his heels, holding the pot between his palms and raising it to the window—how had it clung on, there in the dark, with the soil at its roots shrinking as it dried? He raised it and drew in its scent, which was not of sap or leaves unfolding but something more earthy and enduring. When Eve came in a moment later she saw him in a new and unexpected light, reveling in something ugly and small with the uncomplicated pleasure of a child. It had pained her for reasons she didn't understand, and later she found ways to be unkind.

One afternoon Alex squeezed the seeds from a tomato he was eating, and rinsing them free from their flesh gave them to Walker in a square of white paper. "See what you can make of these," he'd said, and watched disbelieving as under Walker's ignorant care a small vine surged up its wooden cane, and all summer put out dark fruit pointed at the tip like quails' eggs.

When he was thirty Walker had married a woman he'd found in the garden of someone else's house, wrapped in a blue coat though summer had set in a week or so before. She was rather like a mouse, with pale brown hair cut close to her head so that it lay flat and gleaming, and very dark large eyes that darted about and never missed a movement anywhere. Her friends called her delicate but said it laughingly, because although she seemed frail, with her small slender limbs and long neck, there was something steely about her. Walker had teased her into removing the coat, and liked the way she leaned back in her chair with her arms hanging by her sides; he'd liked her clever wry commentary on the party as it unfolded in the darker corners of the garden, and liked buttoning her to the chin when the night grew chill.

He soon discovered that her delicacy was a skill cultivated with some care—she managed never to suffer from anything likely to dull her eyes, but instead developed headaches and fits of breathless anxiety in parking lots and long dull parties, and spent her wages on a man who cleansed her spleen through the soles of her small high-arched feet. There'd been some surprise when they married—those who knew him best suspected him of doing it out of mischief. But Walker inhabited his marriage as if it had been a cell he'd bought and furnished for himself. It required self-discipline and restraint; it left no time for mind or eye to wander; it occupied him with so many small tasks of care and attentiveness that it held in check the restlessness he'd always thought would see him alone at fifty. It required him to be needed, and always to feel that he required nothing in return.

When his firm passed him files for a private clinic whose debts were so heavy the patients were in immediate danger of being turfed out of their beds, he'd flicked through the disordered paperwork with a prick of irritation—nothing was simpler, he'd always felt, than the neat ordering of incomings against outgoings, and the tidy accumulation of capital. The clinic had put its faith in God, and in an accountant of dedicated and patient corruption who over the course of forty years had drained its funding streams into many small channels of his own making.

"You might find it easier," the chairman of the trustees had said, in an apologetic phone call early one morning, "to come and stay a day or so; no more than a week, certainly—we have room after all!—it's the papers, you see—going back years—and to think how well we all liked him! He came to my daughter's christening, you know—I can hardly believe it, and who knows how much of it all is false . . ."

"They don't really need you," his wife had said, her breath smelling bitterly of herbal tea. "Not half as much as *me*"—but he went all the same.

He'd imagined with pleasure a sinister redbrick place, three-storied and deep-shadowed, with gargoyles spitting from the gutters, but St. Jude's was a modern building set around a neat small courtyard, with windows that let in light from the east and an acre of garden. The staff came mostly from the convent and were trained in medicine and prayer—they wore modest wimples so stiff they looked as though they were made of paper and their voices were implacably kind. Inside, the retreat (no one ever said "hospital") resembled a suburban home, with pale floral wallpaper and sofas with tapestry cushions, and a vast television in what the staff called the "lounge." A piano huddled in the corner of the room under a gray canvas cover, every now and then showing a pair of scratched wooden feet, and in the courtyard benches bore brass plaques in memory of benefactors or residents moved on to better things. The patients were largely wealthy and devout, under the care of a consultant who came each week in a cab paid for by the authorities, who had an eye to the scarcity of hospital beds and were kindly disposed to St. Jude's program of gardening and devotions.

Walker was greeted by a pair of trustees who talked in whispers, afraid the patients might overhear and become anxious for their future. He was given a room tactfully distant from the wards, with a pine cross above the bed and a view of the courtyard. He ate small plain meals alone. The task absorbed him, as he'd known it would, and late in the afternoons, content with his work, he'd go out to the courtyard to smoke. Curious, he kept close to the corners, watching staff move in patient circles between the gardens and the long dim corridors hung with watercolors of bluish hills and never meeting their eyes.

It didn't occur to him to wonder why he felt no regret that the work was time-consuming and circuitous, and that he took no pleasure in his wife's occasional calls. Nor did he notice that he timed his courtyard walks by the movements of certain patients, pushing away his work and patting the pocket of his shirt for his cigarettes when he thought he might catch them on their way outdoors. He liked to watch the man who'd stand for an hour or more at the window, tugging fretfully at his beard as though summoning the courage to go out; and the boy with the long eyelashes and amber hair who surely couldn't have been unwell—he was too quick to laugh, and would stand beside the older man lightly touching his elbow and talking quietly as if encouraging him to step out into the autumn rain. Then the women came and brought a change of air—Hester in a coat that smelled of cats and woodsmoke, and Clare, so like her brother; and Eve, who drew a black fringe like a wing across her eyes when he passed her in the courtyard, and was always at the old upright piano. Remembering that music, and how he heard it first through the open window of his room, Walker paused at the wooden bench in front of him, looking out over the dying lawn where Clare dragged her shadow across grass. It had been nothing but an annoyance, that incessant repeating of childish patterns as she disciplined her hands, and the melodies he thought he recognized—he shook his head: he ought to have fastened the window against the sound, and turned back to his papers and the task he'd been set.

Behind him, Elijah opened the greenhouse door. His damp hair was combed into ridges against his skull, and he wore a dark tie printed with swallows. He paused on the step and looked up to the sloping glass ceiling; it was, he'd said more than once, the nearest he came these days to a chapel. He said, "Have you seen him?" and picked a small fruit from the tomato vine. It had been left too long to ripen on its stem, and had split open; the lips of the broken skin were whitish with the beginnings of mildew, and between them showed the translucent flesh inside. He put it in his mouth and burst it against his palate with his tongue.

Walker took a steel tack from the windowsill and began to pick at the black soil beneath his fingernails. "Alex? Not since last night."

"Our new friend John told me all about it, then let me win at chess . . ." He smoothed his tie, and lowered himself into the chair. The cane creaked and shed a flake of paint. "A terrible business—I heard Clare crying this morning, though Hester said there was no need. I would like to see him. I'd like to see for myself how he is . . . they say he doesn't remember it, you know. You don't think he might have . . ."

"I don't."

Elijah smiled, and with his thumb tapped the arm of the chair. "No more do I. But still—he's our responsibility, wouldn't you say?"

Walker unrolled his shirtsleeves, and buttoned them

at the wrist. He shrugged the question away. "You look tired."

"I am. Saturdays tire me—they were always the burden, you see, not the day after. I'd sit up all night waiting for morning, reading and praying until I was hungry. Hard habit to break, after all those years . . ." He tilted back to look at the roof, but closed his eyes against the sun, and tried instead to recall a church he'd seen once stranded on a fen, its roof borne up by angels with cobwebs in their mouths. "And what d'you make of our John?" he said, remembering with a smile how the other man's pale brown eyes had widened with shock under their heavy lids: *we all just assumed you were mad.*

"Oh—John. I don't need to make anything of him. There he is—nothing we can do about it now." Walker shrugged, and Elijah, turning away, smiled and said nothing.

Not long after his last Sunday as a believer, Elijah had held a meeting in the study where he prepared his sermons late into the quiet nights. On his desk *Strong's Concordance* was open at *persevere*, and above it a framed print of Bunyan's Christian making his way to the Celestial City shone behind polished glass. Two of the church elders, arriving in dark suits and black ties as though the very worst had happened, listened with disbelieving sadness; the third and oldest had offered a series of kindly rebukes, but finding them met with silent agreement suggested instead that they pray. Elijah dazedly followed the familiar cadences—*Amen Lord: let it be so, to the glory of Thy name*—and noticed for the first time that his brother in Christ had taken to dyeing his hair.

He'd known it would be painful to remove himself from the pulpit, with its high wooden rails stained darker where his hands had rested those past twenty years, but confronting his wife had been worse. He'd married her for her soft rich voice and her piety, and her faith in him almost matched that in her God. She hadn't believed him at first, and nor had their daughters, though he suspected them of reveling in so unexpected a turn of events—later that night he heard the youngest laughing on a long high note cut off suddenly as though she'd pressed a hand to her mouth. He was being tempted, she said, like Christ in the wilderness: would he give in so easily? He discovered that it was not merely a betrayal of a god too remote to notice or mourn his loss, but of something nearer and more easily hurt. They tried to find common ground; there was none. The best he could offer was a promise to think it over and to pray, if only he could: "I can but try," he said, finding that the loss of faith did not gain him freedom to deceive. He took the bag she packed him, and later found a Bible in the folds of his shirts.

It was a priest who'd recommended St. Jude's to the bewildered preacher, who was unsuited to being alone but had no desire to talk to the faithless (he felt they had the advantage over him, having lost nothing). By the time he'd unpacked his bag in the large low-ceilinged room overlooking a courtyard where leaves spun against the wall, the cavity left when he lost his faith was filled with a weight of fear that grew heavier as the days passed. When asked what frightened him, what always occurred to him first was that he wasn't sure how the sky was being held up; this he knew he couldn't say, and instead took to shrugging and smiling, and gesturing vaguely out of doors. On the second Wednesday in November the visiting consultant, himself a lapsed atheist with a vice for prayer, diagnosed an anxiety disorder and recommended he stay as long as funds would permit. Elijah's wife, patiently waiting for the backslider to return, took their daughters home to Scotland and wrote loving letters every week, in cards showing Bible texts so heavily wreathed in flowers he could never make them out.

Elijah's world dwindled around him. For the first time in his life, no one ever sought his wisdom or advice, or measured everything he did against a Divine standard he couldn't hope to achieve. Life pared down: he slept a little, ate a little, and watched autumn harden the earth. He avoided his fellow patients, not out of distaste but in case the sadness in him would prove contagious, and instead took command of a deep-seated chair set between two windows, where he sat for hours reciting silently the hymns he'd once sung, beating out their melodies with restless hands.

It was there he first saw Walker, smoking in the courtyard on a memorial bench (*It Is a Far, Far Better Rest I Go To, Than I Have Ever Known: Eleanor Mary, 1920–2005*). He had known at once that the gray-haired man who frowned in the shadow of an upturned collar was nothing to do with either the staff or the patients— he kept apart from them all as effectively as if he were sheltered behind panes of glass. Months later, as the two men shared wine with Hester in the blue-lit dining room the other side of the forest, they'd laughed and shaken their heads: "To think," Elijah had said, "there we were, all silently watching, and not a word once passed between us . . ."

At the beginning of his second week in St. Jude's, long before Walker took up his post in the small offices choked with paper, Elijah had been woken in the night by a young man crying. The cries were pitched high and unbroken then deepened suddenly—*What are you doing? Everything would be all right if you would let me . . . you don't need to and anyway I have to get back*—and were silenced as the boy was calmed or sedated. The hopeless echo along the corridor had been unusual enough in that decorous retreat to have kept the residents awake till morning, and at breakfast they ate somberly, watching the door for the newcomer. Elijah had been shocked at the boy's face—"Like an empty paper mask," he said that evening to one of the staff, "like it would crumple if you touched it." She'd fretfully touched the rosary beads in the pocket of her cardigan and said the young man had almost broken his shoulder, throwing himself against the stanchions of a bridge near his home—possessed with fear that its narrow concrete pillars couldn't bear the weight of traffic, he'd tried to bring it down one night when the roads were quiet.

The consultant, coaxed from his practice on a Thursday, prescribed medicine that dulled the boy's eyes until they looked as though they were covered in a film of dust. But he ate, at least, and did no harm to himself or others. With startling speed either the tablets they gave him in pleated paper cups or the calm of the place returned him to himself, and it wasn't long before Elijah found himself waking to the prospect of a sunny face at his door and a hand beneath his elbow in the hall. He discovered that Alex had that trick of the very beautiful, of persuading others beauty must be a symptom of goodness and could be caught by standing close by. And there was general agreement, in the room where the staff drank quarts of tea and out on the allotments where they were planting broccoli for spring, that in Alex it wasn't a trick after all. When the first month had passed, the dullness in his eyes cleared and his good nature looked out at them all—he managed somehow to exist exactly halfway between the patients and the staff, treating them all with instant affection as if he'd known them for years, and couldn't think why he hadn't come sooner. He'd stand beside Elijah at the window with his hand resting lightly on the older man's shoulder and say: "I'm not clever like you and I know I don't understand, not really—but don't you think tomorrow you and I could take one step into the garden, only one, and see how you are?" It was a little like being comforted by a wise child, and never failed to make Elijah think that the next day—or the next, or perhaps the one after—he'd follow the boy out into the courtyard, where the man whose name he didn't know was smoking the last of several cigarettes.

Creaking in his cane chair, watching Walker pat the pocket of his trousers with a sharp decisive gesture and withdraw a steel lighter, Elijah said, "I remember the day you arrived. You looked more miserable than any of us. I remember thinking it looked as if you'd had a headache for years."

Walker laughed: "You were always by the window. I'd've thought the place was haunted only I saw your breath on the glass."

"But I don't remember the women coming—why's that, I wonder?—only that suddenly there they were, and no one was ever quite sure whether they were one of us or visitors . . ."

Walker could remember very clearly the day the women came and the dustcover was dragged from the piano in the hall. But he would not admit it, and turning away from the preacher reached out with his foot to nudge a beetle fretting at the dirt between the tiles.

The three women had come at the end of the second month. Clare with her brother's eyes and hair and her forehead creased with anxiety, clinging to Hester's arm. The older woman—whom Elijah would have taken for their mother had her face not seemed to be that almost of another species—had come wearing such authority that at least three of the staff thought her some director or trustee come to peer over Walker's shoulder as he sat perplexed at the books. Eve, following a few paces behind, unsure whether her old friend would welcome a face he mightn't remember, had knelt on the grass beside the bench where Alex sat, covered her face with her hair ("It was down to her waist then—do you remember?" said Elijah. "And she'd put it tight like a noose round her neck and scare us half to death . . .") and wept all afternoon. When she was done with crying, she dried her eyes and went to the room where residents dozed in their deep-winged armchairs. Pulling the dustcover from the piano she played so quietly that no one woke, though the nurses on duty came along the corridors and leaned in the doorway to listen, inclining their white-capped heads.

All that autumn other visitors could never tell whether the three women had come for the day, or would return that night to small locked rooms in a quiet corridor. Hester would sit with Elijah at the window, saying little but conveying such steadiness and comfort he'd forget to glance overhead and see if the sky had come loose and was bearing down on them. She made herself useful kneeling between rows of winter crops, pulling at weeds and making even the most melancholy laugh out loud. Eve taught some of them to play, and though the staff grew tired of hearing the same childish duets played over and over, no one had the heart to lock up the piano and hide it again under the heavy gray cloth.

Walker would watch from the courtyard corner, making his careful audit of them all. He watched Clare without desire, for the dreadful beauty of her face and her child's smile, and would have liked to sit beside Hester, buttressed by her weight and warmth, and simply hear her speak. Eve he disliked at once for her black sheet of hair and eyes that never missed a trick, and for the music that made him restive and uneasy. He saw the quick light steps that carried her body restlessly from room to room (she took thirty-two paces across the courtyard), and overheard her coaxing laugh, or murmuring in corners with patients who put their hands in hers. Knowing she demanded to be seen and admired, he refused to do so. "He doesn't even know we're here!" she said once, watching him turn away from them one afternoon, his collar turned up against the wind.

In the end it was the piano that sent him over the border into their territory. The sound of it—especially dissonant that day, since some patients were attempting a duet—reached Walker in his airless room. Driven distracted by his hopeless task, he wrenched open the door to the hall, where a dozen or more residents sat quietly waiting for a meal. He'd crossed the courtyard to reach them and his gray hair glittered with drops of rain that fell on his coat as if he'd brought the storm indoors. He slammed the piano lid shut, and the two

women playing—easily startled at the best of times—
only just managed to pull their fingers free. They stared
at him for a moment, then snatching up bags from beneath the broad low stool left the room squabbling with
indignation.

Eve had been sitting cross-legged at Elijah's feet, inspecting a torn nail, her long hair matted at the crown
from an afternoon asleep. The buzz of the disturbed
piano strings reached her as acutely as if it had been the
voice of someone she knew well—she started, leaning
on the preacher to tug herself upright: "What is it—
is something wrong?" Then, seeing who stood at the
door, she said: "Who *are* you, anyway? What are you
doing here—what do you want?" Elijah had looked
at her then, her tall fine body tense with anger, and
thought she'd run to the piano and raise the lid and play
something so insistent Walker would hear its echo all
that day, and later too when he tried to sleep. But she
stood where she was, parting her hair with her hands;
the other man seemed fixed in place, one hand resting
on the piano still and his mouth half open as if he'd forgotten the art of speech. The preacher, whose years in
the pulpit and out of it had made him wise, murmured,
"Oh *no* . . ." and then shook his head and looked away.
Beside him Hester turned the pages of her book, and
Clare put the final pieces to a jigsaw puzzle someone

else had left unfinished. When he looked up again Walker had gone, and Eve was standing with her hands half-raised. When she turned toward him it seemed to Elijah that her face had altered, and in her eyes there was an avid look that troubled him.

In the greenhouse Elijah stood and joined Walker at the window, watching him dig with the steel tack at the soil beneath his nails. The tack slipped in his fingers and slid a little too far between the nail and the flesh; the younger man winced, and sucked at a sluggish bead of blood.

"Give it to me, it's rusted—you'll make yourself unwell." Elijah tossed the nail beneath the bench, and putting a hand on Walker's forearm said: "I know what you have been thinking. I can see it. But I won't believe Alex did anything wrong, and nor should you. You think the worst because you feel responsible, because we brought him here. It was always my job to think the worst of us all—original sin, you know: it makes a man a pessimist. But I think for now we'll believe the best . . . Oh! Here comes Eve, and she's brought us water and ice."

At the end of his second month at St. Jude's Alex forgot what had brought him there. He was young and resilient—his bruised shoulder healed and he couldn't remember what caused the slight ache remaining. Each day he took the tablets they offered, thankful they dulled the elation and misery that had worn him out by turns. He became exhaustingly full of life and went through the wards like an electric charge, helping the residents deck their narrow rooms with dusty boughs of holly weeks before Christmas, insisting on a tree ("I'll fell it myself if I have to!"), helping Eve teach carols which they sang in ragged harmony to the staff.

But early one evening, sitting beside Elijah as they waited for Orion to appear over the courtyard wall ("I tried to teach him the constellations," said Elijah, "but the only one that stuck was the Pole Star . . ."), Alex sat counting the green and white pills he held in his palm and said: "I'm not quite myself at the moment, you know. I'm half of me, maybe not even that. Hester says at least it's the better half, but I don't know if it's enough . . ." He tried to explain to the preacher how it had been before: how he'd felt each crack in the pavements and pebble in the grass through the soles of his shoes, and the blood coursing through each separate artery and vein. The tablets he took with his morning tea blunted not only the edges of his misery, but also muted each of his senses. Sometimes he sat stroking the back of his hand, feeling the slide of skin on skin and wondering if his touch had always been so slight and so brief—surely he'd once felt each ridge and groove in the whorls of his fingertips? He fell to wondering if he were really there at all—here was his hand on the door, here his feet taking turns on the carpet—but what if his place in the world was not secure, like a tooth loosening in its socket?

No one realized he'd begun to fill his pillowcase with the capsules he pretended to swallow, nor that in time he'd begun to persuade others to do the same. "Just like a kind of game," he'd whisper in the corridors, his arms linked through those of other patients as the white-capped nurses passed on the other side: "It can't hurt, just for a day or two . . ." He taught them sleights of hand and tricks to deceive the staff at breakfast and supper, and collected their pills, green and white and yellowish, in the pockets of his jeans. Hester, never easily fooled, saw the merry glint in his eyes harden to a constant glitter, but said nothing, biding her time.

By New Year there was a change of air. Residents grew mistrustful and easily vexed, preferring to sit alone in their rooms and leaving their meals uneaten. No one came to listen when Eve played the piano, and a woman took a sudden and violent dislike to Clare and accused her of stealing her clothes. A young man who had a compulsion to wash scrubbed himself raw with a wire pad he found in the kitchens and was treated by doctors for the wounds on his hands. It was Hester, watching all the while, who finally put an end to it. The force of her character had given her a status she neither sought nor earned, so that when she asked to see the senior nurse she did so with such an imperious lift of her chin that he followed her into the courtyard in a worried hurry. Wringing his hands and hers in turn he conceded that the fault had been theirs—there should have been better procedures in place; they'd failed in their duty of care.

Alex could not stay, nor did he want to—what else could he do but go with Hester to her empty house on the other side of the forest. It seemed obvious too that Elijah should come, and when he'd paused at the door and flinched at the low winter clouds Alex had taken his arm, and it was hard to say who leaned on whom. Walker—his work long done—watched them go, and staff on the morning shift found all their files ordered and annexed, and the cross taken down from the wall.

The uneventful patterns they'd established at St. Jude's were repeated in the house without any particular effort or thought. Letters for Elijah were forwarded and became scarce; Alex ranged through the house painting shabby windowsills and replacing handles on the doors, or sleeping for hours in the kitchen alcove while Hester made the air thick with steam as pans simmered on the stove and too many loaves of bread proved under white cloths.

Eve—who'd returned to her London flat and despised its steel stairs and view of a slow canal—arrived one afternoon with no forewarning, her hair cut short as a pelt and a sheaf of music under her arm. She said to Hester: "I never did find a piano that suited me better than yours," and chose a room from which she could see the long path that led to their door. One afternoon Elijah found her bent over fallen sheets of music, and stooping beside her to pick up a page saw a woodcut of an ape in slippers and a bonnet huddled in an armchair.

"'*Messalina's Monkey*,'" said Eve, vaguely. "Just some old song."

"Is it quite all right? It looks sick."

"Dead, I think—music and monkey both." She took the score from him. "Did you sleep? I didn't . . . that light from the reservoir comes in like yellow water—I dream that it's rising round my bed and the sheets are wet and I'm cold . . ." She shivered.

Elijah laughed. "Can't you just close your curtains, child? Let me take these—I'll walk with you." He went ahead of her down the hall, pushing open the door to the music room and standing back to let her pass. It was winter then, and dark by half past four; Hester had turned on all the lamps and they threw circles of brighter red on the papered walls. Elijah helped Eve raise the piano lid, and pulled out the tapestry stool so she could sit. She bowed and laughed, and bending her head played a swift high run that made an ornament somewhere buzz in sympathy.

"I'll leave you," said Elijah, then, turning at the door, he said on impulse, "Do you ever hear from him? Walker, I mean—I thought you might talk again, you and he . . ." He regretted it at once—her narrow back stiffened, and she lifted her hands from the keys. "I'm sorry, I shouldn't . . ."

"Oh! No, no . . . I did wonder whether anyone knew, or saw—no one says anything here, do they? We'd all rather be in the dark . . ." She played a low chord that put notes where they ought not to be, and Elijah felt it in his stomach. Then she said, "I wish I could explain how it felt, when I saw him that day—it was impossible, I never thought it could happen—he was just a stranger and nothing to me but it was as though I looked up and recognized him . . . Do you understand how troubling that is? And after that what else could I have done, it would be like finding a door half open and hearing a voice you know on the other side and never going in." The chord hung and died in the air. Then she said, very quietly, as though she were ashamed of herself, "Sometimes I stand at the window and imagine him there on the lawn and my throat *aches*, and I lift up my arms as if I could reach him through the glass." Then she laughed, and turned in her seat to look at him. "Sometimes I think I don't even like him, not really; he told me once that he doesn't much care for music—can you imagine!—and that he only wanted me because he knew I could never want him. And I wonder if that's why he's angry with me sometimes, because it wasn't a choice, or something reasonable . . . but I was only ever glad. How could I not be?" She looked down at her hands, and plucked at a shred of skin beside a nail. It tore, and she winced and flicked it to the carpet. "He knows where we are. He knows he can come when he likes. But he won't—he hasn't got the courage." She shrugged, dismissed him with a nod and turned away, then began to dash at the piano with her hands. When, not more than a week later, Walker joined them in the blue-lit dining room one night as though he'd always been there, Eve looked at the preacher across the table and arched her black eyebrows: *Well! Who'd've thought?*

The greenhouse door swung open, and seeing Eve at the threshold with a glass in each hand Elijah stood, watching Walker make a movement with his shoulders that might have been a shrug or a flinch. The preacher smiled behind his beard, and loosening his tie he bowed a greeting to Eve and said, "I am going to find Alex." Behind him Walker knocked a jar from its bench and scattered shards of glass across the tiled floor. "*Gird thy loins up, Christian soldier!*" whispered Elijah. He bent to pick up the largest piece, and went out laughing.

Eve watched him go, then said: "I couldn't find Alex this morning, though I looked everywhere I could think of. Hester says he's all right, and that he slept the whole night through, but how would she know?" She shrugged. "There's nothing we can do but go on like we always have. Oh, Walker—how can you be so clumsy, with such wonderful hands? Let me help you . . ."

II

That same morning John had woken late, the joint of his middle finger tender where he'd gripped the pen as he sat writing until dawn. In the kitchen downstairs Hester had passed him strong tea and toast with honey, then gone out to the garden with a pair of shears, snapping their blades as she went. He thought perhaps she'd avoided his gaze, as though she knew he'd caught her out in something secret the night before, but the idea was troubling and he shrugged it away. He had no appetite, and chewed wearily at the crust for a few minutes, then carried his plate to the sink and rinsed it under hot water. On the windowsill above the sink a housefly washed its hands, and John watched a while then frightened it away. Then he took his plate to the shabby dresser in the corner, where a soft white bundle was fastened by cobwebs to the corner of a shelf. He imagined it seething with small spiders waiting to hatch, and shuddering turned away to sit alone at the long oak table, tracing the name *EADWACER* cut into the wood. Not since arriving at the house had he seen the table empty—on any other morning he'd have found Alex leaning on his elbows and tearing at new loaves of bread, or Clare caressing the spiteful cat. Perhaps I really am alone, he thought—perhaps everything that happened yesterday has broken us up for good, and they've all gone back to whatever's waiting on the other side of the forest. He strained to hear footsteps rapping on the bare wooden floors above, or Eve at her piano, but there was nothing. Having prized solitude for years he discovered it made him uneasy; he stood so suddenly that he knocked his chair to the floor, and went out to the garden to see who he could find.

Up on the raised verge beside the reservoir Clare sat cross-legged, patting at something in the long grass. Between the girl and where he stood the lawn was empty but for a herring gull in the shade of the diseased elm, so white and rigid he thought at first it was cast in plastic or glass. The gull screamed once then turned its head and regarded John, frowning, and shifted its splayed yellow feet.

"*You* again," he muttered fondly, remembering the

gull out on the marshes. In the still air of the garden it was the nearest he had to a companion, and he edged forward with a hand outstretched, feeling foolish but determined to reach it if he could: "Should you be here? Were you invited? I don't remember asking you to come . . ." Its tail was blackened, as if it had been burned or dipped in ink; the bird switched it from side to side and retreated deeper into the shade. The company of birds had been so rare since summer set in that John would have liked to say, "Look! Look at its eye, just like a drop of custard!" but no one was there. Then from somewhere in the house behind him he heard someone laugh; he raised an arm to shield his eyes from the sun and saw movement in the greenhouse. He could just make out, through the green-stained panes above the low brick wall, Eve's black curls above her thin neck, and Walker's graying head. They stood side by side at the window making slow definite movements at something out of sight, and there was a stillness and contentment in their bodies at odds with everything he'd seen before.

He began to move toward them across the lawn, thinking he'd rap at the window and gesture to the gull, which opened and closed its beak as though laughing silently at something just out of sight. He wanted to say, "I think it followed us here, all the way from the marshes," and see if Eve would smile, or even Walker with the reluctant curl of his mouth that he already knew well. But as he came within the shadow of the greenhouse he heard the woman laugh again, not as she often did like an actress obeying her script, but quietly as if it had been a private remark. If John had forgotten by then that he was nothing more than an intruder, the feeling returned with its full force of loneliness and shame. He fell back, and finding himself exposed and vulnerable on the bright empty lawn walked swiftly to a pair of copper beeches that grew against the garden wall. Their black glossy leaves sheltered him as deeply as a curtain might, and pressing into the shade he found he could draw near the greenhouse without being seen. After a brief silence, in which John made out Eve's raised hand pouring soil into a pot that Walker held, he heard her voice carry clearly through the dead air: "He went swimming again last night, you know. I'm afraid he'll knock himself out in the dark, and no one will be there to find him . . ." She turned her back to the window, and John saw plainly through her shirt the sharp bones of her shoulder blades, and between them a darkening blot of sweat. Then she put her hand up to Walker's shoulder, and brushed something from his clothes. "He's taken to John, anyway—I saw them together by the reservoir two nights ago. I followed them down, I don't know why. Perhaps I shouldn't have, but we don't know anything about him, not really, only that he came from there . . . when they came back they were laughing, and John was saying the dam couldn't possibly break—but we knew that all along, didn't we?" John, fastened to the ground by the sound of his name in her mouth, strained toward her. Then she said, "He's very like you, you know," and smiling turned back to the window, making deft movements with her hands at something out of sight. The ease between them fractured and for a while there was silence.

The gull padded scowling toward him and screamed again. The sound startled the pair inside the greenhouse—another of the windows flew open and a small white pebble was flung out. It startled the gull, which gave a weary thrust of its wings, shot John an aggrieved glare and wheeled away toward the reservoir where Alex and Clare lay unmoving on the bright grass of the embankment. It found a rising current of hot air, and rode it out of sight.

"D'you remember being a child and drawing birds so they made the letter *M*?" said Eve, watching it go and bringing her tilted head to rest against Walker's shoulder. "And every house had a chimney, and the sky was a blue stripe with nothing between it and the green earth."

"They say that's how the Greeks got their alphabet," said Walker. "Cranes flew over and made all the letters with their wings and legs. When the last crane in England was shot, it was the end of the great poets." Inclining his head so that it almost rested on hers, he arrested the movement and said, with a return to his usual careless voice, "All nonsense obviously. Give me water—my mouth is dry." John, beech leaves pricking him through his shirt, felt a curious surge of envy: *I'd've told her all of this*, he thought, *if only she had asked.*

"The glasses are empty and there's no more ice. I don't think I ever knew what thirst was like till now— that your tongue could be sore with it, and your lips crack. On the radio this morning they said it would rain tomorrow or the next day or the next, but I can't imagine it, can you? It would be like a miracle."

Walker laughed and said: "*Western wind, when wilt thou blow, the small rain down can rain . . .*" and the words were so unlike him that it was like watching him hand her a gift of something stolen. After that there was silence again, and no movement from the windows. John waited, his bent back aching, thinking of his notebook and all its empty pages. Surely it was his duty now to watch and wait and listen? What else might be said—might she say his name again, with that particular inflection that leaned on the sound as though she were trying not to laugh? Then Eve began to speak in a slow soft murmur, pointing down toward the reservoir at something John couldn't make out. It delighted the man at her side, who, with an impulsiveness at odds with his usual careful gestures, kissed her forehead where her hair parted. She subsided again into the circle of his arm.

For a while John watched them—so still and quiet he thought he could see their bodies fall and rise on the same breath—then shame and loneliness overwhelmed his curiosity and he turned to go. He might have made his way unseen back to the house and the safety of his dark narrow room if the gull had not returned, bearing a grievance. It settled between John and the greenhouse, shook its white haunches, threw back its head and let fly a volley of cries that rang across the empty lawn. Walker straightened, and leaning forward peered through the murky pane of glass. His gaze scanned past John and rested for a moment on the bird, which had begun to dig with its yellow beak at something hidden in the scorched grass, then slowly returned and rested without surprise on the watching man. John began to raise his hand in cautious greeting, but Walker's gunmetal eyes were leveled at him in amusement and challenge. John fell back a step or two and felt the blood gather in his cheeks: he'd been found out after all—he was nothing more than a lonely peeping Tom. He waited for the mockery that surely was coming— for the greenhouse door to fly back on its hinges; for Walker's scorn and Eve's half-pitying contempt. But while he waited, wondering if he would ever be able to exhale the breath straining in his lungs, Walker turned back to the girl at his side and pushing aside the neck of her T-shirt kissed her again in the hollow behind her collarbone with as much deliberation as if he were writing something down. Then he raised his head again, half-turned toward the window, and slid a look at their watcher from the corner of his eye.

Something started then in John, which ought to have started long before, when he was young and might have borne it better. A surge of envy rose in his throat as he watched, and he put a hand to his mouth as if he'd taste not his own palm but the damp white skin at the nape of her neck. All at once, without warning or effort of memory, he saw each small detail of a woman who hours before had been a stranger. The bitten nails at her fingertips and the dry earth ingrained in the soles of her feet were secret and prized—he'd have liked to conceal each part of her from any eyes but his. He could not have despised Walker more if it had been he and not John who'd lied his way to their table. A pain set up very low in his stomach—or not quite a pain but an insistent tugging—gentle at first but which would sharpen later when he lay in the narrow iron frame of his bed, and later still when he expected it least, as if hooks had been pushed through his flesh and were sometimes forgotten, sometimes pulled at steadily or with bursts of malice. That his mind and body together would conspire to such treachery made him gasp aloud; he pressed a hand to his belly as though he could suppress the ache, and turning his back swiftly crossed the lawn with blood beating painfully in his ears. When he reached the long shadow of the house he looked up and saw Hester there at the door with a wine-stained cloth thrown over her shoulder, eating a green apple.

"Dear John," she said, "you really ought not to stand in the sun. Are you feeling sick? I think I have tablets for indigestion somewhere, or a bottle of milk of magnesia: come inside, won't you, and we'll see what we can do. That sort of thing never lasts long."

III

Walker left Eve dozing a while, in their place against the wall where the long grass lay like sheaves of wheat. Always she felt blasted apart, and took time to reassemble: she imagined patting blindly about for each piece, fitting part to part, wondering if there was an alteration anyone else might see.

A cricket hummed against her ear, and she guessed the note it made—something below the middle C, rising and falling, never hitting on a melody. The sun sank mercifully low, and the fringes of the Thetford pines turned black. She wiped at the moisture on her neck, and there was on her hand a scent—thick, sour, urgently sweet—that wasn't entirely hers.

She recalled more often than she liked that conversation with the preacher—*I looked up—I saw him—I was only ever glad.* As a child she'd say: "I never lie, not ever," so often that no one believed a word of it. But she felt it to be true—it was as if whatever she said, she was afterward compelled to believe. She had looked up; she had seen him; she was only ever glad. Glad now, or glad enough, drowsy with heat, drunk on it, the bones of her spine aching from long pressure on the hard earth, a little sore elsewhere. Glad later—glad tomorrow—glad when they fell to mocking? Glad when he said, "You get away lightly: you've done nothing wrong—the price is mine, not yours," glad for the company of that grave new stranger half-hidden behind his beard? *I never lie, not ever.*

Across the lawn the house crept behind the deepening dusk. It was this image Eve had first seen, coming to it when she was hardly more than a child, she a shadow to Alex and Clare a shadow to her: "You won't believe it, Evie—every year she finds another room, and there's a piano so big you could lie underneath it and never be seen . . ."

Eve, watching her parents in their neat small house and feeling she must be a changeling, envied her friend bitterly. Alex—whom the school forgave long absences on account of his feckless mother, whose sister mirrored him so beautifully, who spent summers in a house as deeply forested as anything built by the brothers Grimm—had the life she knew ought to have been hers. She dutifully studied; Alex cheerfully failed. She could not be absent an afternoon without a worried father; Alex came and went as he pleased. She holidayed in trailers whose upholstery smelled of last summer's rain; Alex walked barefoot in overgrown gardens and drank wine from the bottle. He once attended double maths in a velvet coat with filthy red braid at the cuffs; she could not pass the doorstep without her tie re-knotted and straightened with a fretful pat. How was it possible to attain greatness when her mother bought a pair of china dogs to flank the fire with its three electric bulbs, and her father was afraid to enter restaurants? She refused the first invitation ("Go on, you'll like Hester, and she says the piano's yours . . .") with a lie about the Spanish coast, but accepted each that followed, suspecting rightly that her parents were relieved to be spared her scowl, and her hands that mutely practiced Chopin on the plastic tablecloth.

Over the long summers that followed, Hester's other visitors, their numbers dwindling, instinctively sought permission from the frowning green-eyed girl before they raised the piano lid. By eighteen—and the last of the summers, as it turned out—Eve no longer thought of her talent ("Remarkable, actually," said her tutor, crossly, finding envy inescapable) as a gift—"I am not gifted," she said, willfully absurd: "I am *cursed*." It was not that she resented the hours spent on the hard stool, her eyes sore and her back developing its long ache— she'd no more have complained about those than about hours spent drawing breath. What she meant (though she could never explain) was that the music she sank into seemed so frightening, so sublime, so terrible, that on rising again the real day had nothing in it to quicken her pulse. On she lived—a friend here, a lover there, all the ordinary crises of life—feeling everything muted. There seemed such a gulf between her self and the astonishing power of those eighty-eight keys (something that left her visibly shaking, or lying awake feeling it still in her hands), that every note she struck seemed a small lie. "I've *felt* nothing, *done* nothing, *seen* nothing—I'm a long pause, an empty bar: I make no noise at all . . ."

If she'd willingly cast about for means to make herself the music's proper match, it would certainly never have come. Instead she grew detached from how she played and how she lived, not much caring about either. Then the house and everyone in it receded for a time— Alex moved on ("We'll always know each other, don't you think? And I'll know where to find you . . ."), the little group dispersed. Calls and postcards grew scarce, and the career promised for a decade or more seemed always imminent and never more than that.

Alone in her flat a few winters on, the house in summer seeming something she'd once overheard, a rumor reached her: that beautiful boy had broken in pieces; he was locked up, and mad as a March hare. Her first thought—so shameful it was never admitted, even to Walker, with his trick of probing for her worst—was that she envied him plummeting so far and so fast. *If only that madness had been mine, think what I could've done with it . . . !*

She never really knew why she'd gone to find him in that curious institution, its residents politely mad. It was love, or curiosity, or both; but love won out the moment she saw him diminished on a garden bench in winter, with his dull eyes half-closed against the light, and his slow-coming smile.

And then there was Walker, and he was entirely familiar, and utterly strange, and she couldn't help it, and she was only ever glad. *I never lie, not ever.*

IV

I've come down to the greenhouse. There's no one here. I can smell the fruit on the tomato vine left to get too ripe and something's moving under the bench. All the shadows are thick in the corners and I can almost believe the dead plants are putting out new leaves. The air in here is so moist I can feel it on the pages of the notebook; I've opened a window and the tilt of it gives me two moons to write by. I don't know what the time is.

Sometimes I remember Elijah leaning across the table in his room with the torn-up Bible all over the walls, saying, "We all just assumed you were mad!" and I laugh—it delights me, it's so absurd. And then I think: here I am in a stranger's house, writing in a stolen notebook with a pen that isn't mine, a liar of a man laughing to himself down here alone in the dark—who'd blame them for thinking me mad?

Then I feel the ache in my side that won't go, and think: is this the first symptom? Is this the beginning of madness, this pain under my ribs real as anything I've ever felt, though no harm's been done? Perhaps whatever kept my mind and body separate has severed and I'll never divide them again . . .

When I went up to my room after I'd been watching the greenhouse I found this book and wrote down her name, in the margins and on empty pages at the back, and every time I see it I smile though I don't know how I can with the shame of having been caught out and my heart <u>hurt</u> like a muscle too long out of use . . .

Eve

Eve

Eve . . .

No. <u>No</u>. Let me make an account of what Hester said this afternoon. She'd been out all morning buying food, and the kitchen was full of vegetables and meat and bottles of wine as though we're under siege. There were a dozen green apples on the table, and someone had put them in a circle around the string of cowries that Clare had brought back from the beach, reminding me of a picture I saw once of tokens in a burial chamber. Hester sat me down and gave me some disgusting medicine in a glass—like ground-up chalk stirred into milk—and said it would stop me feeling sick, and I was so grateful for her company I wouldn't have told her what the real trouble was even if I'd known. She said, "I'm sorry for what you saw yesterday, out on the marshes—I wouldn't have had you witness that for the world. Not for several worlds, indeed!"

I had a mouthful of medicine, which was so thick it choked me, so instead of answering I settled for shaking my head and shrugging. I think she knew what I meant—she leaned forward and patted my hand twice as though she were grateful and said, "I knew I needn't worry—I knew you'd understand. He's not himself, you know. A beautiful loving lad but never really free from what troubles him . . ." She shook her head, and lowered her eyelids so that her whole face took on a resigned and mournful look. But I couldn't shake the feeling that there was something a little satisfied in her as she surveyed the aftermath of the day's events and the unease that had prickled under my skin the night before returned. Then she got up quickly, with a dismissive sort of gesture as if she'd dispensed with that subject and was ready for the next, and started to fill the kettle. "He will be fine, now—none of us need ever think of it again. Let me make you tea—my mother told me it's the thing for this weather."

When she returned to the table with two mugs over-full with strong tea, she said, "Did I see you coming from Elijah's room the other night? I hope you didn't find his room too odd!" She smiled, and this time it was so frank and mischievous, and so plainly affection-ate at the mention of the preacher's name, that I forgot my unease and would've told her anything she asked. I said I thought it a very practical way of forecasting a storm, and that made us both laugh. Then she said, "Have you spoken to him much? Or have the others told you why he wouldn't come with us to the sea, or even go down to the reservoir?"

I told her that we'd talked a while in his room, and said, "I don't understand. How can I? I never had faith. I can't imagine that mislaying it would be such a calamity."

"Nor I," she said. "But there it is. He's afraid of every-thing, you know"—she flung out her arms and ges-tured toward the window, where a bright strip of empty lawn showed below the blind—"Afraid of everything. Just—everything." Her hands dropped to her lap and fidgeted there. I said, "Heavens above," and she smiled.

"Hells beneath, more to the point—though really we ought not to laugh."

I told her how I'd seen him on my first night, standing at the window looking up now and then as though waiting for the sky to fall in, and as I spoke I realized I'd begun to remember things as though they'd happened years before.

"Yes, that's just it—waiting for the sky to fall in!" Hester sat up straighter and pushed back the hair that was falling into her eyes. "That's just it—the sun in pieces like a broken plate. He wasn't always like that, of course—he had that kind of faith so solid it wasn't faith anymore, it was certainty. He didn't *believe* in God any more than you believe in me. I'm here, aren't I?" I smiled at that, because with her heaviness and with her eyes that see everything there's something about her you could worship.

She told me he had believed that the God who made Adam out of dust and clay knew Elijah, of Clapham, south London. "Believed that he'd counted the hairs on his head, watched him sleeping, helped him put one foot in front of the other without falling over." She shook her head. "He had a wife and three daughters— did he tell you that?—and they weren't any less faithful than he was. Maybe you catch it if you breathe it in, like a virus. So there they were, just think of it—the hand of God turning the world on its tilted axis, and at the same time seeing to it that your cold improves and you can find a parking space when you need one, and you always have money for the gas bill."

I imagined Elijah's arms pierced and threaded for a puppe-teer's strings and shuddered, spilling my tea. As though she'd seen it too, Hester said, "Oh, I don't think of it that way, like a great eye in the clouds. I think it was more that God was everywhere, being beautiful and good, holding up the sky. I remember Elijah saying once he only needed to look at dandelions growing by the side of the road, greasy and black with exhaust fumes, and there was the evidence of God. His was the Kingdom." She shook her head in admiration and pity.

I don't know why, but I began to feel impatient with the old preacher, that he had let a fine and wise mind be broken over something so slight. What difference was there, after all? He had not seen God then; he did not see him now. I said, "Well, what happened, then? How do you lose God? You go out one day and he's no longer there in the weeds?"

Hester drew together her heavy gray brows. "It's easy to laugh, of course," she said reprovingly. "I did, at first. But if you could see how afraid he is—he said to me last week: It's the Last Times, Hester! Then he remembered he didn't believe in all of that anymore, but that was even worse. The world ending because its Maker has decided it's high time is one thing. It collapsing without purpose or meaning is quite another."

Then she shrugged and went on: "He told me about the day it happened, though I'm not sure I believe it. I'm not even sure he believes it himself, but I suppose we all explain ourselves as best we can. Did he tell you about his study? Sometimes I think he misses that more than his family—his books and papers, the pictures on the wall, the cup he always used for tea in the morning. He had his desk against the window, so he could sit there and look out at Creation. Every morning he went to his study, and didn't come out until the afternoon—except on Sundays, when there wasn't time. Every week he had three sermons to prepare, or four on special weeks, and for hours he'd sit at his desk reading the Bible, or books about it. I imagine you'd believe in anything, don't you think, if you read it every day?"

I smiled then, thinking of one long wet summer when my brother had learned the language of Tolkien's elves and wouldn't answer to any name but Celeborn. I said, "I think you probably would."

"He told me it happened like this. One Sunday morning he'd just finished dressing in his suit and tie and was going over his sermon notes. It had been a hard year for some of the congregation and Elijah knew his duty, and wanted to comfort them. So he found out somehow—he might have counted, for all I know—that in the Bible the words *be not afraid* or something like it come three hundred and sixty-five times." She drained the last of her tea with a gulp and said, "Do you understand? To Elijah it meant only one thing: thousands of years ago God had personally seen to it there'd be enough comfort to go round for every day of the year."

I felt again my annoyance, disappointed that a man I liked so much could have been so simple and childish in his reasoning. I said I thought it seemed to me a kind of madness, turning everything over until it fit an idea. She smiled and said, "But don't we all do the same? I believe that right this minute we are circling the sun, because I have been told it's so—I've no evidence for it myself. Anyway, there it was—proof he'd been made in the image of God, and the path he walked had been planned before time and was fenced off from danger. Then his youngest daughter came in—they all wore long skirts, you know, for the sake of modesty—and asked him what it was he planned to say, and he told her about the comfort of God, and the three hundred and sixty-five days. And d'you know what she said?" I shook my head, and saw that her lips were pressed together as if she were trying not to laugh. "She said: What about leap years? What about leap years!"

She saw I didn't understand and, lightly slapping the table, said, "Don't you see? The girl said, 'You've always told me God has ordered everything for my own good. But every leap year, when winter has gone on too long and we've forgotten the feel of the sun, there'll be one day when there's no word of comfort from God. And either he knows about leap years, and means us to be unhappy and afraid one day every four years, or he doesn't know about leap years after all. So either he's unkind or he's ignorant, and either way he can't be God, because to be God you must be perfectly kind and perfectly wise . . .'"

It seemed so absurd that I felt a curious mix of anger and amusement, until I remembered how grave and sad Elijah always seemed, and how he restlessly drummed on the arm of his chair. I said, "So for want of a nail, the Kingdom was lost?"

"It was like the little tap on the glass that makes the window break. He told me she kissed him on the cheek and went out laughing, thinking nothing of it, and he went on sitting at his desk. Outside daisies were growing on the lawn, and suddenly they weren't carefully made things there to make us good, or whatever it is he'd been telling the Sunday school children all those years, but just accidents. Happy accidents, but accidents all the same." She peered at the dregs of her tea. "He told me it was like falling out of love. He looked and looked at the weeds in the garden and the sun in the sky and so on, and tried to summon up—what: love? Awe? I don't know—and it just wouldn't come. It must've happened to you, John. We've all felt it. Love going for no reason you can think of; a face you thought beautiful becoming ordinary, or worse." She turned her black eyes on me like a light, and it was as though I were being searched. I thought of Eve's face and of the small details that had become essential to me—the tooth that's set a little farther back from the others, the blue veins in her lowered eyelids—and could not imagine it would ever be ordinary. Afraid she'd see the change in me I stood and carried our mugs to the sink. On the windowsill someone was growing a seedling in a plastic pot; it had been left too long without water and the tips of the leaves were withering. I scooped water from the sink and dribbled it into the pot, imagining the seedling growing plump and straight as I watched. Behind me Hester said, "Of course he couldn't just put his Bible under his arm and go up the pulpit steps. He might be afraid of everything, but he's no coward. So he found St. Jude's and after that came here, and once he was over the threshold he never went out again. He's alone for the first time in his life and he's terrified."

I asked what his family thought of his change of

heart, and she said, "Well—they're confused, I suppose. They write. He writes. They'll go back to London soon and he'll join them if he can—but what then? They're still living with a light shining on their feet and a lamp on their paths. And now he's just like you and me, stumbling around in the dark, trying to find his way."

She stood up with a groan and joined me at the sink. Touching the leaves of the seedling on the windowsill with her little finger, she said, "One of Walker's attempts, though I doubt it'll survive the summer—and here he comes with Eve, laughing about I don't know what. Are you all right there, John, or are you feeling sick again? The medicine is on the table—pour yourself another glass."

After that I went down to the garden again, where lawn gives way to brambles and nettles. Everywhere bindweed had taken hold, so that it looked as if all the trees were blooming at once. I crouched a while on a piece of wood that must have sheared away from one of the pines in a violent storm, and put my head in my hands. I tried to order everything I'd heard and seen since the day I arrived, but nothing would fit, and underneath it all was that curious ache in my side, as though I'd been injured and not felt the blow. When I lifted my head and saw Alex a little distance away, I was glad: he at least seemed to see me directly and clearly, and even to have need of me—not as he thought I was, but as I am.

As I came nearer I saw that he was crouched intently in the shade of a sycamore, with his back turned to me and his head bent. He'd taken off his T-shirt, which lay beside him in the grass, and I could see the bones of his spine and the birthmark like a shadow on his arm. The sycamore was shedding its spinning keys all around, but Alex didn't look up—whatever it was he'd found on the ground absorbed him completely. Some distance away the cat huddled at the foot of the tree. Its eyes were swollen almost shut and it was licking its paw.

When I reached him, I coughed once or twice so I wouldn't startle him, and he looked up sharply like a child caught out in something they ought not to be doing. He said, "John!" with surprise and displeasure, and then frowned and bit his lip, and looked down at the grass between his hands. I said, "I wasn't looking for you, no one sent me. I only came because I wanted to be alone too." Something in the grass moved, and I came closer. When he looked up again the displeasure had gone and he looked both guilty and wretched, but determined to continue with whatever he was doing. He muttered, "Go away," but not with any conviction, so I came closer still and crouched beside him. When

I saw what he had between his hands I think I cried out, because he said, "I'm not doing anything to it, not anymore!" and shifted away from me a little.

Pinned to the ground by his forefingers, a large moth struggled in the grass. It was far larger than the pale moths I'd seen in the dining room, or beating against the lamps in the room upstairs—it must have measured seven or eight inches across its wingspan, though I suppose it would have been less had it not been stretched between his fingers like a man on the rack. Its wings were thick like velvet and the color of a horse chestnut, marked darker at the joint where they met its fat body, and with one blurry marking of white at the tip, as though they'd been touched with chalk. Its legs looked far too frail to bear its weight, and every now and then they twitched with a horrible imploring gesture. I couldn't see its eyes, only a pair of strange flat antennae that looked like the soft furred leaves of sage. As I watched, Alex suddenly grasped its right wing between his thumb and finger as though he were going to tear it apart; the moth arched and convulsed its body and although it was silent I thought I would hear it screech, or hear the tearing of its wing like a piece of fabric. I said, "Stop—what are you doing—Alex, how will it fly, if you take one of its wings?" I wanted to pull his hands away, but the moth revolted me and I turned my head so I wouldn't see its distress.

He gave a long explosive sigh and his whole body sagged; I thought he'd pitch forward and cover the moth with his chest. He loosened his grip, but its wings were still pinned to the grass, and the creature lay quite still for a while as if it had given up hope. Alex muttered to himself, and dipped his head to his shoulder to wipe the sweat from his forehead and what I thought might have been a tear. I said, "I can't hear you—won't you tell me what you're doing, so I can help?"

He said, "You thought I could do it," and gave me a sullen look that was nothing like the bright frank smiles I had come to expect from him.

I said, "Let it go now, Alex—nothing good ever came of hurting even something so small," and all the while I was thinking, I thought you could do what— who have you been talking to? What have they said?

He looked again at the moth between his hands, this time with a puzzled frown, as if he couldn't remember how it had come to be there, or what he might have been intending to do. He withdrew first his right hand, and then his left, with a show of care that was a little like fear, as if he thought it might rear up from the grass and beat its wings blindly against his face. It did not, only lay there twitching a wing. Alex turned his back on the moth, drew his knees up to his chest and buried his face in his arms. His shoulders convulsed once with a sob, then he suppressed his tears and instead drew in a series of long slow breaths while I sat beside him and patted his shoulder, even putting my arm round him and pulling him against me, as if I could steady him, saying that he hadn't done any harm, and that of course no one need ever know what I'd seen.

After a minute or two he calmed himself, and lifted his head. When his eyes met mine he seemed himself again, as if he'd reassembled who he'd been the day we went together to the reservoir. But he said again, rue-fully, as if he knew I wouldn't want to hear it, but felt it should be said: "You thought I'd be able to do it, didn't you? You thought I could hurt it. I did try, and not just that, I tried earlier too . . ." Unconsciously he looked over to the foot of the sycamore tree, where the cat with its swollen eyes still nudged and licked at its paw.

I felt a little cold then, wondering what he'd been doing while I sat with Hester at her table, but still I let my arm rest on his. I said, "Never mind that—never mind what you have done or what anyone has done—I would never think you could hurt anything else, you know. What made you think so?"

He drew away from me then to reach for his T-shirt, which he pulled over his head. It was stained with dust and pierced with the stems of dried grasses. I stood and saw that the moth had gone.

"She told me. She said she heard you say so, to the others: that you thought—yesterday—I might have done it, only not remembered . . ."

I was bewildered and angry; I think I can bear anything but being made out to be what I'm not. I said, "Who? Who have you been speaking to?" all the while thinking: Let it not be Eve, thinking so little of me and doing so much harm.

He said, "Well, Hester, of course!" as if it were foolish of me even to ask. He smoothed his T-shirt, and looked at me again, and I saw in his eyes a mixture of challenge and uncertainty. "And I remember nothing, not really, only the boat and the boy wanting to see it, and the way I could hear the water coming up through the grass and the mud and the gulls screaming like men a long way away. So I thought maybe I did hurt the boy—if John thinks I could have done, even John!—so I came here away from the others to be on my own, and thought I would try, and see if I had it in me. And I couldn't, not really, though I think the cat might limp a while; I couldn't even pull the wing off a moth, just an insect, so what would I be doing with a child? John? What would I do to a child when I can't hurt even an insect in the grass!"

I'd've liked to put my arms around him like I did when Christopher was a boy, but I think he hated me a little, for believing I thought so badly of him, so instead I stayed away and said, "I never thought so. Not ever, not when I saw the woman on the path, or later when we all talked it over on the way home. Hester—" Pity for Alex was erased by a burst of rage, and it was a while before I could speak again. "She's mistaken, Alex—that's all. She must have misheard. No one believes it of you, and neither do you, and you must think of something else now."

He stood for a long while with the sun putting lights in his hair, and the sycamore keys spinning from their branches. Then he bent to pick one up, and said, "I saw a woman once who wore a necklace with one of these in silver hanging from a chain. She said inside the silver was a real one and I remember thinking that it seemed wrong, walking about with something dying round your neck." Then he smiled, in the old frank way I knew, and said, "All right. I won't think about it anymore. I'll put it away somewhere, and won't take it out again. That's the best way."

So we walked together across the grass, and our

shadows were long and reached in front of us, and behind us the cat came slowly. We could hear Eve playing the "Maple Leaf Rag" much too fast, and Clare calling from a window upstairs, and as we walked I repeated to myself over and over, under my breath: <u>put it away somewhere and don't take it out again.</u>

Eve   Eve   Eve

Western wind, when wilt thou blow?
The small rain down can rain.
Christ! That my love were in my arms
And I in my bed again.

I have known that poem all my life!

I can't write any more.

Monday

I

O n the morning of the sixth day John woke to find a gray haze gathering at the lower edges of the sky as though all the fields east and west were on fire. He stood watching a while at the window, buttoning a shabby blue shirt he'd found, wondering if the haze would rise and gather into storm clouds.

The changing sky made him ill at ease; certain he could not sustain the deceit another day and would soon be leaving, he wanted to memorize every detail of the house, as he'd once memorized poems to be recited in front of a class of boys he never came to know. Alone again in his ordered flat, would he remember what he'd seen and heard? Surely he'd forget the flight of steps and the green door, the blue lights in the blue room where they ate and the lichen that crept across the terrace stones?

When he made his way downstairs he paused in the cool dim air of the hall. It stretched ahead of him, surely far longer than he'd first thought, and a bunch of keys hung in the lock of the front door. He heard a quiet dry rustle from somewhere very near, and looking up saw a strip of wallpaper peel from the damp plaster behind and droop toward the floor. Stooping to smooth it back against the wall, he saw for the first time the design of tangled leaves and branches, with small birds caught in the dense undergrowth. The pattern was so deep and dark he wouldn't have been surprised to hear little furtive movements, and he stared for a long time at a goldfinch until he was sure he saw its black eye blink. He smoothed his palms against the paper, hoping it would fasten back against the wall, imagining Eve painted there and hiding in the thicket. He felt again the painful tugging in his stomach, and was so absorbed in imagining her there that when she passed by a moment later he thought he must have summoned her.

She said: "I have to talk to you," and put out her hand. It hung in the air between them an inch from his sleeve. The thin bluish skin was pulled tight over the strong musician's bones, and there were blue shadows between the knuckles. Her voice had lost its particular musical tone—it was terse, all seriousness. The hand crossed the last inch between them and touched him lightly on the forearm, and the ends of her fingers were hot.

John met her gaze with difficulty, remembering Walker's long sly glance at him as he had drawn her closer against his side—had he told her they'd been watched? Was he going to be mocked all over again?

"Oh?" said John. "What is it?"

"I need your help." It had the rising cadence of a plea; he made a half step toward her and brought his own hand out from his pocket, then, not knowing what to do with it, instead reached up to smooth his beard. She said, this time leaning on the first word, "We need your help."

"Of course," he said.

"Of course. Well . . ." She glanced over his right shoulder, where down the stone step the kitchen door stood half-open, then brought her eyes up to his with the snap of a key fitting its lock. "But no—shall we go for a walk?" She slipped away down the dim hall, beckoning as she went, and he followed the flash of her bare feet on the carpet.

Outside, as he watched her walk ahead of him on the scorched sharp grass, John felt again the change of air, as though there'd been a disruption overnight. The stillness now wasn't like the calm before a storm, which would surely be a gathered sort of stillness, like a muscle bunched before a blow: this was complete inertia, and more unsettling than a lightning strike.

She stood waiting on the lawn beyond the blighted elm. Around him the sun picked out every shallow fissure in the dried-out earth, and gave each blade of grass its own black shadow. But as he came near to her, he saw that she stood within a bluish shadow slowly moving. It spread for several feet around her to a blurred edge, and shed a softer light on the fine white lines of her face and hands. She beckoned—"Hurry up!"—then lifted her arms above her head. The sky, empty for thirty-five days, was punctuated by a single cloud moving east, shedding white air at its fringes, as solitary as if it puffed out of the chimney stack. John came and stood beside her in the shadow. "You wanted to tell me something?"

"Yes, I did." She drew her black brows together.

"Is it Alex? Did that woman call again?"

"No . . ." She waved distractedly, as though pushing the stranger out of their dark circle. "It's not that. At least, it's not quite that. Look—I want you to take this." She reached into the pocket of her shorts and took out a small envelope. It was stamped, though the stamp wasn't franked, and had been opened and closed several times until the pale brown paper was soft. Above the address the name ALEXANDER was written in poorly made capitals.

"Another letter," said John. The sight of it depressed him, and he took it reluctantly, as if the stupidity and spite inside might be contagious.

She nodded. "I found it yesterday. It was under the doormat. You don't need to look at it"—John had half pulled out a folded piece of newspaper—"it's more of the same, another drowning—Wales this time, I think. Oh, John—who'd do this? Who'd be so childish?" She plucked at the fragile skin on her throat and left it mottled and red. "I want you to hang on to it. In books they burn them, don't they? But don't burn it. Keep it. Maybe we'll need it sometime. No good my taking it—Alex comes to my room too much, so does Clare; and I don't want Hester to know. Did she speak to you this morning? About anything important, I mean?"

John shook his head, pushing the letter into his back pocket and feeling it weighing on him.

"It's her birthday tomorrow."

"I remember. Sixty."

"And not for the first time! Anyway—there's supposed to be a party. You'll be the only guest—no one else is invited. There isn't anyone else to invite."

For a moment he was tempted by the old polite uncertain formula—"Oh, well, that really is kind, but I don't"—but it was much too late for all that. Eve, seeing his hesitation almost before he felt it, raised an eyebrow and said: "It's all planned. More than she knows. Clare has made a cake." She threw him a glance from under her fringe: *you and I will both be kind, however awful it is*. It made him complicit, and gave him far more pleasure than it ought to have done. She lifted the curls from the back of her neck in a gesture he'd begun to recognize, arching her back as though testing the strength of her bones. Her shadow reached beyond the circle of shade, and then retreated as she lowered her arms.

"And Walker wants to show a reel of film he found in the attic: *Hester As a Young Woman*. You can't imagine, can you? I think she was an actress for a while. She has the voice. I suppose I'll play something. Elijah might sing. Everyone has to do something. We did it once at St. Jude's you know . . ." She looked anxious for a moment, as though she were afraid she'd been insensitive. John felt a pricking at the back of his neck and flicked at it, expecting to dislodge a sucking gnat, but it was only a leaping nerve.

"What I need *you* to do," said Eve, stretching her bare foot ahead of her so that her long toes, already dirty, poked out of their circle of shade, "is talk to the woman. She wants to call it off—says it wouldn't be right to celebrate. *In the light of events.*" She shook her head. "It's no good. I know what will happen because I know Alex better than her—he'll spend all day down by the reservoir, feeling miserable and guilty because it will be his fault there's no music and no one's dancing, and no one ate his sister's cake. We have to carry on as if everything is all right because if we don't, it will never be all right again—especially after yesterday. You agree?" It wasn't really a query, but he nodded, glad again to be needed. "There's no use at all my speaking to her. You'll have to do it. You have a beard. It counts for something." So she couldn't keep the mockery from her voice for long—the seriousness briefly left her and her speckled eyes roamed speculatively over his face. Then, as if regretting the change, she became grave again and said, "Please do. Please. She'll listen to you."

"Of course I'll try. But what shall I say to her? Has anyone ever changed her mind about anything at all?"

Eve turned to look at him. In the mild light of their little dark territory on the lawn her eyes brightened. *Oh, but they're not green after all, not quite,* he thought. *I'll have to think what color they are, so I can write it down.* "Don't you understand?" she said, then paused, smoothed a damp curl from her forehead, and said:

"Look, she doesn't mean what she says. Nobody ever does! Dear John, you're so like Clare. Don't you ever pick things up, and look to see what's underneath?" *Dear John,* she said, on a cadence like the music he heard her playing at night, and without warning there began an insistent pulling in his stomach, so like the painful drawing of the day before that he put his hand to his stomach as though he felt sick. Then, afraid she'd notice, he arrested the movement, and instead hooked his thumb in the warm brass buckle of the stranger's belt.

"She doesn't mean it—oh come on, follow me, it's getting ahead of us: there must be wind, up there!—it's just she needs to be heard saying the right things. She must have the correct feelings. D'you see? After all, how could we love her if we thought her selfish? And of course if we're made to plead with her, and tell her how loved she is, how we can't believe she can be sixty, how there's no one in the world quite like Hester, for she's a jolly good fellow—well, then she'll know we love her." John nodded, thinking not for the first time how changeable they all were, and how mistaken he'd been on almost every score. He said, "If I do this can I be excused from any—from any kind of performance?" He said the word distastefully, then to show that of course he looked forward to her playing, if to nothing else, he added, "Because I've no talents at all, you know."

"We need a listener: they also serve, who only stand and wait. Now then," she touched him lightly again above the elbow, and this time her fingertips were cold. "Thank you . . . I don't suppose you imagined we'd all need your help like this—but I promised Walker this will be the last thing we ask of you."

The mention of the other man soured John's pleasure, and he crossed the lawn slowly, setting his back straight like a soldier doubting orders. He looked once behind to see Eve standing in her diminishing circle of shade. She was waving down the garden toward the valve tower—someone was coming to meet her. Ahead of him, the house in shadowed replica on the lawn tilted toward him, and at the kitchen window Hester stood half-concealed by the lowered blind, her forearms plunging and withdrawing at the sink.

"More tea?" she said when he opened the door, rehearsing how best to begin.

"Yes—thank you." He watched her move heavily between the table and the draining board. Something bubbled on the stove and gave off a thick floury scent he couldn't place. She dried a teacup on her apron, which was not clean.

"How's Alex?" he said, implying that she alone would have the full story. The kettle sang on the hob.

"Tired, I think." She poured the water too rapidly into the pot and splashed her arm without flinching. When she came to the table with two overfull cups, scald marks bloomed on the back of her hand. "He didn't sleep much. He was down at the reservoir most of the night, though I don't think he went in the water. These days I think he just likes to be there. Hard to say by now whether it's a curse or a comfort. It's always the way, don't you think," she said, getting up to stir the pan on the stove, "after a while our troubles are the only thing we have that never change and we wouldn't lose them, even if we could."

She sat opposite him in a chair that groaned under her. Her fine black eyes were hooded with sleep. "She called once more last night. There's really nothing wrong with the child. He'd come to more harm at school! She didn't thank us, not quite, but everything's cleared up. There is—what do they say, on the news?—there's no case to answer."

She sucked thoughtfully at her cup, and a thick drop spilled from the rim. "Best just to leave him a while. Best to let him sleep. There's all the time in the world for talking." She began to sort through the piles of letters and magazines and books on the table, impatiently clearing a space, then returned to the stove and left her tea to stain a long-outdated headline *(Austrian Excavators Return Empty-handed).*

The table was scored with knives and burned by pots hurriedly set down. John traced the words NOT THIS TIME with his forefinger, and felt a chill pass through the damp high-ceilinged kitchen. Behind Hester, in the cool green-painted alcove where the night before Alex had sat with his knees drawn up under his chin, Elijah was silently reading. Some trick of the light, coming at him from the windows and the harsh strip lights set in the vaulted ceiling, doubled his shadow in the recess, and his heavy down-turned head was reproduced over each shoulder. Leafing through a paperback, he caught John's surprise at the title and smiled. "Not exactly required reading in the seminaries, eh?" *Hume: On Suicide* said the cover, in a pretty typeface unsuited to its subject. "You've read it?"

"I went in for that sort of thing," said John, gripping his teacup. "When I was young." The handle was loose, and rasped when it was touched.

"This sort of thing?"

"Oh, you know. Thinking." Stirring at the stove Hester let out a quiet blow of amusement.

"Ah." The preacher stroked the embossed paper

cover. "Perhaps I'd've done too, if circumstances had been different. I find it hard to disagree with now. Might even have done then, when I lay down in green pastures so to speak." He smiled ruefully, and John could not have said whether he regretted having once been content to lie down, or having gotten up again.

"I preached on it, you know," he said. "Very often. Popular sermon subject, nice and clear-cut: ending your own life goes against the will of God, which is that we would all live long enough to serve Him. *What is the chief end of man?*" he recited thoughtfully: "*To glorify God, and enjoy him forever.* But this man here"—he shook the slim white book—"says that if one day you went out walking, and saw a rock rolling down toward you, no one would condemn you for stepping aside and averting your death, and diverting the will of God. Taking your own life in that case—isn't it just the same, like putting your finger in the path of a raindrop on the window and changing its course? The raindrop will carry on rolling, because gravity tells it to; it'll just take a different path." He shrugged, turning back to his book; and John, relieved of the need to reply, turned back to the kitchen table.

"Have you seen outside?" he said, tense with the burden of a duty not yet carried out. Hester bent over the pan on the stove and breathed in its steam. When she lifted her face it was blotched and wet. "Looks like the storm's coming."

"Oh?" She brought the pan to the table and sat opposite him, thoughtfully stirring. *I hope that's not lunch*, thought John, looking at the thick translucent liquid with distaste. One final bubble burst weakly on the surface and left a shallow crater. "Good. I feel like my bones have been boiled for soup." She caught his gaze and laughing said, "Oh, this isn't soup, you know. It's glue." She reached behind to the dresser with its chipped crockery stacked on the shelves and brought out the bald china head and shoulders of a handsome man. His eyes were open and all over his brow and scalp were written the qualities of his character, which must have been a trial to his friends: *Blandness, Order, Mirthfulness, Combativeness*. The white packed bundle of nesting spiders' eggs John had seen fastened to the shelf the day before had burst, and several black dots scurried, frightened, over the mouth and nose. Hester blew them away, scooped her middle finger into a pot of Vaseline and smeared a thick layer of jelly over the glazed features. Then she said, "Tell me how you are. I thought last night you looked tired—could you take this? Don't let it stick."

John took the pan from her and stirred the thick

paste with a wooden spoon. "I'd walked a long way," he said.

"But you feel rested, besides the walking and—well, the other business." She pursed her lips as if she'd tasted something sour. "I'll know I've failed, if you don't feel more peaceful now than when you came. It's why you're here, isn't it? And you know we've all been saying how well you look. Just get rid of that dreadful beard and you'd look a boy again!" She took a yellowing sheet of newspaper from the top of the pile nearest her, and began to tear it into narrow even strips. "They were saying so, the girls. Just the other night."

"Oh yes, completely rested," said John, who'd never felt so drained of blood and good humor. "Completely rested. Very peaceful." He stirred the glue into glossy whorls, and taking courage from his sudden skill at dissembling said: "I must say, I'm especially looking forward to tomorrow."

Always alert to changes of air, Hester shot him a look from under the thick gray curls on her forehead. "Thank you, I'll take it now." He passed her the heavy pan. "Tomorrow?"

"I thought you said—did you say tomorrow was your birthday? Might I get a glass of water?" He went hurriedly to the sink. *And did Eve say so too*, he wondered, running the tap to draw cooler water, *did she* really say *I'd look like a boy again*—does she *think of me when I'm away from her in other rooms?* That his mind could wander so easily to her made John ashamed, and he let the flame on the stove come too close to his wrist. In the slot between the windowsill and the edge of the blind the lawn showed bright uninterrupted green: the solitary cloud had burned up.

At the table Hester dipped a torn strip of paper into the glue, and ran it between two tight fingers until a gobbet of paste dropped off. Then she took the wet paper and laid it over the blind white eyes in front of her, pressing it into the sockets with her thumbs.

"Yes, tomorrow and tomorrow and tomorrow." She shrugged expansively, and dipped another piece of paper. Some kind of actress, Eve had said, and John saw it now: she didn't talk so much as deliver lines.

"But I'm undecided—well, you can advise me, I'm sure!—about what to do. Things aren't quite right, somehow. You know the feeling, John, that you might get shaken off your feet and fall over?" Looking not in the least like a woman afraid of falling, she smoothed the wet paper onto the forehead in front of her.

It's *papier-mâché*, thought John, *like my nephews make. Must they all be so much like children?* "What is it? What are you making?"

"A mask. For tomorrow, if we go ahead, like dancers on a sinking ship."

"*Nearer my God to thee,*" sang Elijah from the recess.

Hester picked up the glazed white head, turning it from side to side so that the shadows beneath its eyelids made it seem to slowly blink. "What would he tell me to do, I wonder, about this damn party tomorrow? He looks a wise old thing." Laying the head and shoulders down she said, "Well, perhaps we *should* go on with it. It might take his mind off things." John looked at the glistening strips of paper covering the blind face from eyes to chin. The mask would be too small to cover Hester's coarser face, with its heavy pads of skin at the jowls and underneath her thick unplucked eyebrows.

It struck him that all the childish things they found to do—the mask and the packets opened in the garden, the long meals in the close hot dining room, the childish trips to the coast—were just a series of distractions, because they were terrified of what their idle hands might find to do. But all the same it was soothing to sit quietly, taking pleasure in having done as Eve had asked, watching Hester's freckled hands dip over and over into the pan of glue and hearing behind him the slow turning of pages from where Elijah sat. However fierce the sun outside, the kitchen was always cool:

rivulets of condensation ran down the pale green walls, and the stone-flagged floor gave off a rising chill. John watched a daddy-long-legs creep across the floor, and instinctively drew in his feet with childish disgust. Out in the corridor a door was furtively opened, and after a pause—*The wind through its branches is calling to me*, sang Hester, and began to prize open a tin of black paint—footsteps receded upstairs. Perhaps it was Clare, and he was warmed by the thought, and by knowing that her feet would already be dirty, and that she would have in her pocket the cowries she'd found the day before. It might have been Walker, too, gone up to meet Eve in some small hot room he'd never seen; and at the thought John reached out with his foot and slowly pressed the daddy-long-legs into the cold stone. It left far larger and blacker a smear than its thin limbs ought to have done, and John turned back to the table.

The paper mask was almost complete, a thick gray layer of wet pulp through which columns of black type were still visible. Tilting his head, he made out what he could: *revealed Martha Day, 61 . . . strengthening in the east . . . suspended over allegations . . .* then was arrested by a length of paper laid across the bridge of the nose perfectly horizontal so that it demanded to be read. The headline was truncated: *FOUR FEARED DROWNE—* , and accompanied by a photograph.

Only a part of the picture remained, but it showed plainly a swollen river breaking its banks.

A dreadful thought began to gather from the corners of the room. He drew a thin breath in through a mouth dry as sand, and all the while Hester went on singing (*With soft whispers laden . . .*), dipping into the pan and carefully pasting on strip after strip until the flooding river was covered. The chill rising from the floor enveloped him and he shivered violently, looking away from the mask to the newspapers piled on the kitchen table. Pages had been neatly cut to remove whole articles or photographs, and in one or two places columns of type remained, so that he could see repeated over and over the same few phrases: *drowned . . . lost at sea . . . feared lost . . .* "Oh, *no*," said John, in a voice of childish dismay that he later regretted, because it committed him to a course of action from which he couldn't turn back: "Oh, no . . ."

Hester looked up from her handful of soaking paper, and met his shocked gaze. It startled her: she began to scrabble with the pile of newspapers on the table, piling them on a chair out of sight. Her hands shook, and the papers fell onto the floor. She stooped to pick them up, but hurt her back, straightening with a groan and leaning against the table. The name *EADWACER* scored into the wood showed between her spread fingers, and she tried to cover that, too. If John had at first not quite believed what he saw—that it was she after all who'd been so foolish, and so spiteful, shoving scraps of paper into envelopes like a school bully—everything she did showed her guilt clear as a brand on her forehead.

John shook his head, and felt at first relief—there'd been fault here all along, and deceit, but it was not only his own. Then came a quiet fury as he pictured her sitting at the table at night, while everyone upstairs slept on stomachs full of the food she'd cooked, folding stories of drowning into envelopes she wrote on with her left hand. He imagined her leafing through the book concealed in its cabinet drawer, mouthing the unfamiliar names—*Weland, Deor, Widsith*—then finally *Eadwacer*, to be remembered, and written in the dust upstairs when the others were occupied elsewhere with their games.

We ought to be made to wear dunce's caps, he thought, wiping at the salt sweat that had suddenly gathered in the hair at his temples, *to've been so completely duped*. Hester began wiping her hands on the dark blue dress where it pulled across her heavy thighs. She said, "No, no—it's all right, it's all right." They were the same soothing words she had used to pacify the distraught woman on the beach the day before, and he also stood, poised somewhere between pity and a

rage that had begun to settle in a cold knot in his stomach. Then he remembered waiting by the reservoir
while Alex prepared to swim out, and how white the
young man's back had been as he'd plunged into the
water, and rage won. For a moment he couldn't speak,
and then he said, "But it isn't all right, is it?" Leaning
toward her, he stabbed at the newspapers. "What have
you done? *Do you know what you have done?*"

"You don't understand . . ."

"There at least you're right—I don't." With effort
he took hold of his voice, which had lifted with anger
to the opened window, and brought it down almost to a
whisper; behind him Elijah had dropped the book, and
resting his head against the curved wall was sleeping.
"I don't. And I don't want to."

"Sit down, won't you? Please sit down." The deep
voice had changed to a hesitant pleading, and her fine
dark eyes were enlarged with tears. John suddenly felt
tired and rather sick.

He sat down. "It's too late for all that. Haven't
you seen him, out there every night? He says he sees
it, whenever he sleeps, everyone carried away by the
water . . ."

Hester fretfully smoothed a strip of newspaper across
the high bridge of the porcelain figure's nose. She looked
so like a chastened miserable child that he started to

laugh, then remembering the preacher sleeping in his corner quietened, and traced the name cut into the table with an outstretched finger.

"It's so stupid, so spiteful," he said. "So like a child . . . But no—a child would be ashamed; might do it once, perhaps—but not over and over again . . ." He stopped, seeing again the scene on the path through the marshes and Alex's uncomprehending silence. "Yesterday when we came back from the sea, I saw you looking at Alex, and I thought: why does she look satisfied? What is she thinking that she could be smiling after all that's happened? I didn't understand it then, and I don't understand now. Is it that you hate him? But how could you—how could anyone?"

The woman pressed the back of her hand to her forehead, heavily beaded with drops of sweat that stood on the skin without falling. It was so very like a well-rehearsed gesture of distress that John pushed on, determined to make her face things: "You should be ashamed of yourself. Aren't you ashamed?"

"Oh, I've been ashamed all along," she said, as though exasperated at such a foolish question. "But after a while you get used to the shame and it becomes part of who you are. It was sneaking and stupid, yes, you're right—it was just like something someone like me would do." She put her head in her hands, her coarse gray hair falling forward to show a white neck far more frail and slender than he'd have thought. He was afraid she'd begin to cry, with heaving shoulders and ugly gulps for air, but her tears came silently so that he heard each separate drop landing on the table. He said gently, "I suppose it's quite funny, really. I nearly laughed, when Eve told me about it, and showed me the letters. I thought: it might be some sort of joke. Nobody writes anonymous letters. This isn't a *novel*."

She gulped, and it might have been either misery or amusement. Then he said, "But I don't understand why you did it. It doesn't make sense. I don't understand at all." She raised her head from her arms. Without the authority and warmth she applied to her face as carefully as powder, she appeared to him very young, and it brought a sudden reversal to his anger.

"There's nothing so wrong it can't be put right," he said, remembering how the words would console Christopher like an arm across the shoulder. "And this'll be an end to it all now." Hester picked up the phrenologist's head and surveyed it, biting her bottom lip. "You're very kind," she said frankly. "Everybody says so." John, unwillingly moved by this, coughed and said: "When did all this start?"

"Oh, I can't remember. I can never remember the times of things. It's staying here that does it, I think—

it might be fifty years ago for all I know. I might be young again. I might be as old as my grandmother." Setting the head down again she caught John's look of censure and said, "All right. It started about six months ago, I suppose. Not just this . . . I've made him believe he does things, says things, and can't remember . . . I even let him think he might have hurt that child—after all, perhaps he did."

John shook his head, appalled: "You don't believe it. You don't, and no one ever could . . ." (Between Alex's outstretched hands the brown moth flexed its wing.)

"He was going to leave me!" Gazing down at the table as though she could make out in the knots and whorls of the wood grain the image of his face, she smiled, with the old slow-gathering beam of warmth. "He was getting better, every day he was here. Everything I did for him made him go a little further away, and I realized that soon I wouldn't be hearing his voice in the hall, or coming up from the garden. Then one night I found him sleeping out by the reservoir, because he'd tired himself out from swimming, and I realized that as long he was just a little afraid, he'd need me. There's no other reason. I've got nothing else to give—I can't charm. I've never been admired. I was never that kind. People like me don't find affection coming our way—we have to scrabble about for leftovers."

"I see," said John, and thought that he did—of course a childless woman alone in a house that smelled of damp and too much furniture polish would love a boy like Alex. He imagined her calling him "son" with a slip of the tongue, and saying to her friends, "I couldn't have loved him more if he'd been my own flesh and blood. Not if he were my own!"

But when he looked at her again, her head hanging low as she traced a shape on the table in front of her, her smile was secretive and coy, as though she were thinking over a private pleasure. She was blushing, too, color gathering at the base of her throat where the skin hung in a double fold under her chin, and spreading up to her forehead. In a moment of clarity that made the kitchen seem brightly lit he realized that this ageing woman, in a stained dress that always smelled a little of stale sweat, had fallen in love. He said gently, "I see."

She lifted her head then, firing a black look at him between narrowed eyes, as if she realized what he'd seen on her face and was challenging him to say more. "I think I understand," he said, faltering a little, "I know what you've felt . . ."

"Oh, what would *you* know," she said. "How could you *possibly* know?" He began to nod—her scorn was familiar, and he knew what she meant: that he'd nothing behind his ribs but books in hard covers, and nothing in his veins but ink. But then she made a furious gesture toward him, and he realized with a burst of mirth that this was not what she meant. She'd mistaken him for the other sort, who needn't scratch and scrabble for affection, but found it coming their way when they weren't looking.

He was so thunderstruck by the idea that he slumped against the hard back of the kitchen chair, and listened with his eyes half-closed against the facets of hers.

"What would you know about it? Do you think I don't know what they think of me—old and ugly, with a face that could curdle milk! I dress like this"—she plucked furiously at the old blue dress and he heard the small rending of a seam somewhere—"when upstairs in locked cupboards are clothes with flowers sewn on the breast, and I can't even touch them because my hands are too rough and the fabric is too fine and it catches on my nails . . ."

The heavy lids of her eyes lowered, and she said, "I didn't do all this because he's young and I'm old. It's because I'm ugly, and he's the most beautiful thing I've ever seen. Every time I look at him I feel myself grow older and uglier, until I've dried up into nothing. And all the while he gets brighter and better and further away, and it's so unfair, because I'm not stupid, I'm not unkind. They say you get the face you deserve, but I tell you, John, I never earned my ugliness. All my life I've watched those women with faces they're proud to show and bodies that deserve sunshine and I *hate* them, because they're cut from the same cloth as him. And there are days I forget myself, because my eyes are the only ones that don't see me—I look out and see beauty and think I take part it in then remember I am so different I might as well be a dog in the street, and I have never been desired, and it is beyond me to imagine it . . . and I'll never tell him, even though I don't want anything in return, because what's really cruel is that no one for a moment would believe that a woman like me could fall in love like everybody else."

John would have liked to say that it wasn't true, but wanted desperately to repay her honesty with his own, and he saw as plainly as if the notebook was on the table between them the words he'd written down: *ugly is the only word that will do.* They sat in silence for a long while, and then she said eagerly, half-reaching across the table toward him, "You can still help me, if you want to. It would be helping him, you see, most of all, and I know you'd do that if you could."

"What can I do?"

"There's more—only one—oh, God!" She covered her face with her hands and almost laughing said, "I can't stand to think of it, could I really have been so stupid? There's one more and you must help me look out for it, get to it before he does, or one of the girls— they like to take him things: they go to his room and I hear them laughing together." Her lips compressed with envy and John, not knowing it, mimicked her, remembering how the boy had taken Eve's hand, and with his thumb wiped dirt from the crease in her palm.

Then Hester stood and smoothed her dress with slow deliberate movements and said with her old authority: "It's only eleven o'clock and the post never makes it here till noon. Won't you help me, John? I can't stay there by the front door all morning, but they won't notice you and what you're doing. You can get to it, can't you, before he sees it?" She began to pull drying newspaper from the white head on the table, balling it up in her palms and tossing it deftly into the bin beside the sink.

Then, turning to him again, she said quietly, "You won't understand this, a man like you—I can't imagine you feeling anything you didn't choose to feel, just when you chose to feel it—but you see I didn't know when it started how far I would go."

John stood up in his borrowed clothes, and accepting the hand she stretched out said, "Of course I'll help. It's an easy enough task, isn't it? Even for a man like me." She smiled and gathered the newspapers on the table into a sheaf in her arms. "Thank you. How glad I am you came!" she said, and went out with her arms full of torn newspaper.

They won't notice you, she'd said. John had forgotten Elijah sleeping in his corner, so that when the russet head came suddenly out from the alcove his heart, already restlessly beating, convulsed behind his ribs.

"Oh, the poor woman, poor woman," said the preacher, fanning himself with the white-covered book.

"I'd like to kick her down a flight of stairs."

"No. No, you wouldn't."

"All right. I wouldn't. But why not poor Alex? Why did you think of her first—didn't you hear it, don't you know what she's done?" In the vaulted kitchen his voice rang high with indignation.

"Let's make tea. It's her solution to everything, you know." Elijah stood at the sink filling the kettle, lifting with one hand the blind over the window to look down the bright garden. "Oh, I heard. But poor Hester all the same. It's maybe not the saddest thing I ever heard, but sad enough."

"I don't want tea. It's much too hot. You ought to despise her now, much more than I do—she's been a liar. Isn't that a sin? Or did you give up the idea of sin when you gave up God?"

The preacher shrugged, and striking a match moved his fingers idly in and out of the flame. He turned and with a mild half smile said: "Certainly she's a sinner, if you want to think of it like that. But if you'd believed like I always did that the heart of man is deceitful above all things and desperately wicked, you're never very surprised when people turn out to be liars and cheats. That's the trouble with you atheists: always so optimistic. What surprises me isn't that we sin, but that we manage a single good action in all of our lives." The kettle screeched, and turning off the gas he added with a spread of his hands, "Well, that's what I would have said a year ago. Amazing, isn't it, how easily it still comes? So yes—poor Hester, and I think you pity her too, don't you, or will soon enough. After all"— he turned to John with a wry smile—"haven't we all lied?"

John nodded twice—*oh, a hit, a very palpable hit*— and from somewhere in the garden came the sound of someone weeping.

II

We've all been outside watching clouds being blown inland. The sky's been so empty so long they seem terrifying things that might swell until they swallow up the whole world. We didn't talk much, only watched to see if the rain would come, but in the end we grew bored of waiting and came indoors to sleep, and I can hear doors closing all along the corridor, and the click of lights being switched off.

I'll go on trying to write them down, though I'm all in the dark, a character at someone else's mercy. Sometimes I imagine Tolstoy sitting at his desk with his notebooks spread in front of him, drinking tea from a samovar, or vodka if it's going badly, and I think how easy he had it, always knowing what was coming next. He could tell you what Anna Karenina wore for dinner, all the while seeing steam from the train station puffing out between the final pages.

All morning I watched for that final, foolish letter of Hester's, sitting at my old post at the foot of the stairs. Every now and then when my legs grew stiff I walked up and down the hallway with my hands in my pockets, looking at the wallpaper, sure I'd see birds moving if only I looked hard enough. Hester told me they wouldn't notice what I was doing, and she was right, though I didn't like to hear it said. They're having a party tomorrow and they're all occupied with something or other—Clare passed me on her way to the kitchen carrying a box of candles to decorate a birthday cake, and I heard Walker swearing in the dining room, trying to get an old film projector working so we can all see Hester when she was young, although you can't imagine that she ever was. Elijah went straight up to his room singing something so melancholy I was glad when the low notes gave him a coughing fit and he had to stop, and Eve was playing her scales over and over in the music room at the other end of the hall. I watched for an hour at least, though it's hard to tell here how time passes, but nothing came through the letterbox. After a while, as I grew restless, I heard footsteps in the music room and Eve put her head round the door.

I hadn't seen her since she sent me away from her shaded patch on the lawn to talk to Hester. But I must have been thinking about her all along, because when I saw her face I thought how different it was from how I'd remembered it, but at the same time how familiar her mouth seemed to me, never quite closed, as if she is always about to sing or eat . . .

She looked up and down the hall until she saw me waiting there at the end, and when her eyes met mine I thought, so this is what they mean by a piercing stare. I swear I felt it perforate me, go through my borrowed clothes and my skin, between my ribs and through my liver, heart, spleen, kidneys, whatever's packed away in there, and pinion me to the wall. It hurt, you know, or I thought it did—I wanted to look away because I could feel my cheeks burning, but I couldn't because I thought even if I did, all I'd see, in front of me and behind me, would be those same clear eyes hunting me out.

Sometimes I think that if I had my way I'd wake up tomorrow and would never have seen her—would never have heard her name, and never would hear it either. So I don't understand why it was that when she opened the door and beckoned to me I forgot about the letter and my promise to Hester, and followed her as dumbly as a dog.

The music room feels as though it must be the hottest part of the house—it's a trick of the red-painted walls and the yellow and orange lilies Hester puts on all the tables. The lilies weren't fresh when I first saw them on the second day, and by then were giving off a kind of animal scent, sweet but with something like flesh underneath it. When I brushed past, the pollen left stains on my sleeve as dark as dried blood.

I asked her why she wanted me. It never occurred to me that she might have wanted my company—I thought maybe she'd have some impossible task to test my strength or good humor, and ask me to take the piano out into the garden, or paint the room white to cool her down. But she said, "It's nothing. I'm bored of these scales. Why don't you sit?" The piano stool is made for duets, I think—it has a tapestry cover worn through in the center and is just wide enough for two. She was wearing denim shorts that would have looked better on a boy and her legs were sunburned. I said: "I've got things to do, you know," but she looked as though she thought it was very unlikely, began to play a melody and asked me what I thought of it.

I hated it. It was brutally sad and sweet, and so obviously supposed to be moving that it made me determined to hate it even more. I told her it was lovely, and she smiled so suddenly it made me blink. She said, "No, it isn't. Try this one." Without looking at the keys—she plays with her head tilted down and to the right, as though she's seen something wonderful out of the corner of her eye and can't quite catch it again— she played something else. Her hands hardly moved at all—there were just sly shifts of her fingers sliding on the keys—and the notes were pressed together in dark low groups I'm sure I felt as well as heard. If there was a rhythm I wasn't aware of it—I felt displaced, watching her from a great distance, borne up by the notes, suspended above her. When she stopped I felt myself falling through the sudden quiet back into my seat, and realized I'd been bending low over the keyboard, watching her fingers so closely she must have felt my breath on the back of her hands. She laughed and said, "Better?" and I said, "Much better," and waited for the old blush to start up underneath my beard, but it never came.

In the end her hands got tired from playing. She said, "Thank you. I hate to play alone. It's like talking to yourself all night, and then I realize my arms are aching. If someone's here I can go on and on without stopping." Then I asked her why she went on playing with aching arms, and she said, "It's because everything's such a muddle, and then I come here, and it never fails me. Look"—she played a scale so swiftly I couldn't really see where her fingers were falling—"it's the same, every time, and your ears strain for it, and then the end you long for comes." With her thumb she played the final note again, and I knew what she meant.

I said, "I can only make sense of things when they're written down. Sometimes, when I feel confused and in the dark, I think if only I looked hard enough I'd see words in their proper order, and I'd understand everything better."

She didn't laugh at me, but nodded and smiled and played that final note again, sinking her thumb onto the key so that the sound rang out around us. She said rather eagerly, "Yes, yes—I understand, I do: you have words, and I these eighty-eight keys, but the effect is the same . . ." I remember looking at her from the corner of my eye; her face was turned away from me, the skin so white it was almost blue, and drawn taut over the high bones of her cheek. I looked at my hands and I don't think I'd noticed before how slack my own skin was, and how ugly the black hairs on my wrist.

Then I said, "What will you play tomorrow night, for the others?" and she asked me what I would like her to play and I said anything, I didn't care. Then I touched her wrist and said, "Tell me what you're doing here."

She looked at my hand for a long while, then said, "It's a very good piano."

Since then I've wondered what could have suddenly made me incautious and unwise. Maybe it was the fault of the music, because it had been honest and true and meant only for me, and it made me think: Maybe I matter after all. She had started to withdraw from me behind the hard glazing of her green eyes, when just a minute before her head had almost touched my shoulder while she played. I heard myself say harshly, "None of you ever tell the truth, do you? Tell me what you're doing here. You could practice anywhere, someone like you—why won't you tell me?"

"Why do you need to know?"

"I wouldn't ask if you all kept me at arm's length where a stranger should be, but you don't. You show me pieces of yourselves when you want to and never the rest. Is it because of Walker? What's his real name, anyway? Walker! Does he think he's in a film?"

"You're not a stranger now." She smiled at me, and it was the sort of kindly smile I imagine she might have given an impertinent child. I'd've preferred her to get up then and leave me there, but instead she made that gesture of lifting the curls from the back of her neck, and said, "No one ever uses his first name. It's so unlike him. It doesn't fit."

"Why are you smiling? You hate each other."

"Oh." She looked hurt. "How could you think that?"

She slowly played a chord that I knew, because she'd taught me, was in a major key.

"I saw you with him yesterday."

"I know. Walker calls you Peeping John." This made me miserable with anger and humiliation. I looked down at the clean sunburned lines of her legs and the narrow hips on the piano stool next to me. She said, with a flat detached voice as though she was speaking about someone she didn't much care for, "It was a long time ago now and not worth speaking about. Of course at the time I thought it was"—she flicked idly at the piano keys—"I wish we could come up with another word: this one's gotten all worn out!—I thought it was love. But it broke everything up and spoiled things I thought would never be spoiled and in the end I was left on my own.

"I disappointed everyone. They tell you, don't they, that there's no right and wrong these days. We've all grown up, put that sort of thing behind us a hundred years ago. But there'll always be some things they won't let you get away with and even the words for them don't change. Infidelity, adultery . . ." She shrugged, and the words with their hard consonants were like the snicking of scissors through paper. I remember hearing then a sharp metallic sound out in the hall that might have been the rattling of the letterbox or something dropped in the kitchen doorway and I thought: I ought to go, I've asked too much, I don't want to hear any more—but my hand was still on her white wrist and it looked suddenly very frail and thin.

I said, "But Hester didn't leave you alone, or Clare," and she said of course she hadn't.

"Don't you know her at all? She's a child, a young child, she never knew or saw what everyone else did." Then she looked across at me, and although I don't think she meant it unkindly I thought it was mostly contempt that made her eyes glint under their white lids. "You're not so different from her, are you, John? You watch and watch but you don't understand any more than she does and you've had twenty years longer of living." Then she said, "I want you to understand because I don't want you to think badly of me, and because you asked." Then she said, frowning and pausing between her words, examining them before they got to me: "If what happened back then—if it was all for nothing, just because I was foolish in the same banal uninteresting ways we always are, then it was all just a waste . . . but if something comes out of it, if I can love him now or make him love me, then it won't have been a waste after all—it won't have been foolish and destructive but something good." She laughed and said, "Elijah would probably tell me I'm trying to redeem my soul."

I said, "He was married then—and is he still? Where is she . . . why doesn't she come for him? Don't you care about her, or wonder how bad the pain was when she knew what you had done?"

She smiled at that, and said, "I never think about her. I don't even know her name. What has she got to do with any of it? Could I change what I felt for the sake of someone who I'll never meet?"

I could see the sense and the cruelty in it, and it troubled me—I wanted to think only well of her. And all the while the heat made my head ache, and I kept hearing as clearly as if it were just outside the open window the two of them laughing at me as I hurried away from them across the lawn. So without much truth and with no kindness at all I said, "You must know he doesn't love you. He's laughing at you all the time and you can't see it. It's humiliating for you, following someone, being here because of them, I'm ashamed for you. And besides he isn't anything, he's just a man who's getting old with gray in his hair. He knows nothing, he's not kind to you, I've never even seen him make you smile . . ."

She said vaguely, "You're hurting me," and when I looked at my hand on the piano stool, I saw I'd been gripping her arm all along and had left an imprint of my thumb below the sharp knuckle of her wrist. Though I was hurting her she had not pulled away, but instead drew closer: she almost leaned on me—I could feel her shoulder on mine, and when I looked up her face was tilted so that when a tear edged from beneath her eyelid it ran back into the black curl behind her ear. When she spoke again her voice was low, murmurous, almost a monotone, as though she were an instrument being played and a single note, low and soft, was drawn out again and again. She said, "I'm afraid of not being wanted—I would rather it be him than no one."

When she had finished speaking she didn't quite close her mouth, but left her lower lip loose, so that I could see where the flesh inside became smooth and bright with moisture. The pressure of her shoulder on mine grew more insistent—I thought perhaps she was reeling in the heat and might faint; then I looked again at the black lashes lying on her cheek and the half-open mouth and knew that I was being mocked all over again. It was just like her, that pretense at a kiss, or the beginning of it—I imagined dipping my head to hers and feeling laughter on her breath, and imagined her laughing later with Walker as they walked on the dark lawn sharing one of their cigarettes. I pushed her away and without looking back went out onto the terrace where the stones burned the soles of my feet . . .

There's someone outside my door!

III

John closed the notebook and pushed it underneath a folded newspaper. In the band of light below the door a shadow showed of someone waiting there. He cupped a hand behind his ear and could just make out, above the beating of his heart, the visitor's shallow breaths. He stood cautiously, pushing back his chair, which skittered on the bare uneven floor and fell with a crash. The breathing on the other side of the door ended on a gasp, and there was a long anxious silence in which John imagined each of his fellow guests standing in line along the corridor. *They've found me out,* he thought, darting on bare feet to press himself against the wall beside the door—*Elijah told them I lied and they've come to send me away.*

On the other side of the door, the indrawn breath was

suddenly exhaled with a sigh. It was a woman's voice, and he thought: *It's Eve—it must be, who else would come so late,* and imagined the bruise darkening on her wrist. Low in his stomach, spreading up to make his throat ache, all his confusion and loneliness sharpened into a single clear impulse to have her nearby. He put his hand flat against the door and left it there, as though instead of unpainted wood he had under his palm her sunburned neck, her thin hands with the nails bitten down, her black curled hair that had smelled, when she sat beside him at the piano, very faintly of oranges. Her breath came now with unnatural steadiness, like someone who'd had to be taught how to do it, and he began to match his breath to hers, drawing in the air as she let it out, fancying it was the same, that in him were particles that had passed down her throat and been warmed by her blood. Then she tapped politely three times on the door, and without pausing—if he did, he'd go back to bed and draw up the covers until he couldn't hear the knocking anymore—he pulled the door open.

Standing back as though she'd started to change her mind, clutching a thin dressing gown high at the neck, Clare stared at him with a clear shocked gaze.

"Oh," said John. The longing receded, scooping him hollow. He leaned against the door frame to steady himself.

"Hello," she said. She stepped forward and John saw the gown was printed all over with strawberries and too short at the wrists, as if she'd worn it as a child. She'd wrapped the red cotton belt twice round her waist and tied it, exactly in the center, with a neat bow.

"Clare," he said, as though to be certain, and then: "Is everything all right? What's happening? Is it the dam?"

"Nothing," she said, "nothing's happening." Then, making her voice lower and softer than it ought to have been, she added, "Nothing's happened yet. Let me come in?" He stood aside, bewildered, and as she passed he smelled sweet alcohol on her breath, cherry brandy perhaps, something a child would drink in furtive nips when parents were away. She went and stood beside the window and he looked up and down the hall, bewildered, as though he'd see all the others standing laughing in their doorways at some prearranged joke, but it was empty and unlit. He closed the door and stood with his back to it, gripping his left hand with his right to reassure himself he was awake.

The girl looked curiously around her at the bare tidy room. "What is it you do up here all night? I see your light on sometimes."

"Come away from the window. Are you unwell?"

She put her hand up to the cotton gown at her neck.

"I'm okay. Do you read all night, then? Eve says you're the sort of person only ever happy with their head in a book."

"Does she?" John watched her uneasily. Realizing that his eyes were on her, the girl reached up with her right arm and began lifting the hair away from the back of her neck, arching her back as she did so. She was mimicking Eve in a parody as unconvincing as a schoolgirl in her mother's shoes. Then she plucked at the red cotton cord at her waist: the dressing gown fell at her feet and she stood facing him, naked and afraid. Her imitation of Eve—of the tilt of the head, and her long restless back that flexed and stretched at the dinner table or on the piano stool—was so absurd John would have laughed had she not bitten her lip like a child trying to be brave. He'd have liked to say, "What are you doing?" but knew she wouldn't have been able to answer, and when he put out his hand and rested it on the outcurve of her hip it wasn't desire or curiosity that moved him most, but pity. She flinched, and wondering if his hands were cold he said, "I'm sorry," and stepped away from her toward the window.

He could see all her flaws and defects: a picked mosquito bite on her shoulder above a smear of blood that hadn't been washed away, and the plump uneven flesh on her thighs. At the side of her left breast was a birthmark the size and color of a copper coin, a remnant of the constant shadow cast on her brother's arm, and when she reached up to dash impatiently at a fly troubling her, the hair under her arms was the same dark amber as the thick plait she drew over her shoulder.

Moving toward her, John put his right hand on her breastbone, and fitting his thumb to the hollow in her throat felt her blood beating. But looking down he saw that her eyes were very like her brother's, and dark with apprehension. It made her seem a child again, and he shook his head violently, as if denying something, and stooped to pick up her dressing gown.

"Don't you want me?"

"If everyone always did everything they wanted . . ." He shrugged, and spread his arms in apology and dismay.

"Oh . . ." She considered this without rancor or hurt pride, the way another woman might have done, then obediently pushed her arm into the sleeve he held up. "I see what you mean." Then she clutched her stomach. "I feel sick."

"How much did you have?"

"Two glasses, big ones, and it tasted of currants. I don't like your beard, I can't tell if you're smiling."

He wrapped the belt twice round her waist, fumbling with the knot. "Well, I am."

"But I can't tell."

"All right then, I'll shave it off." She nodded, then looked with disapproval around the small neat room, her hands shoved into her pockets. He wasn't sure what he ought to be feeling—ashamed of himself and embarrassed for her, perhaps—but felt a steadying rush of affection, nothing like the painful drawing he'd felt when he thought it was Eve waiting on the other side of the door. He finished tying the belt at her waist, drawing the loops until they matched precisely.

"I saw you with Eve, earlier," she said reproachfully. "I looked for you all morning but couldn't find you. I've made a cake for Hester. I thought you could help me put the candles in, but you weren't anywhere I looked. Then I heard her playing the song she always plays when she wants someone to like her, and I knew you'd be there, so I went and looked, and there you were."

The song she always plays, thought John. The hollow place in his stomach deepened. Clare kicked the nearest of the boxes. "Why haven't you unpacked?"

"I'll do it tomorrow."

"Can I sleep in here?" Outside, the light above the tower dimmed in the brightening air. "It's not long now till morning . . . Can I lie down just here? I won't make any noise." She lay politely still on the edge of the bed, tucking the dressing gown around her hips and watching him expectantly, so that sitting elsewhere would have been stranger than simply to lie beside her on the thin mattress. John took off his shoes, and stretched out beside her. The raised edge of the bed pressed them together, and her hair was caught up with his on the pillow. After a while she said, "When we shared a room and I didn't like the dark, my brother told me stories."

"It's quite light in here," he said, but the long line of her body next to him was still with expectation.

"What story shall I tell you?"

"Tell me yours."

"Oh . . ." He shifted, and caught the eye of the painted Puritan, who was trying not to laugh. "I haven't one worth telling. Ask for another."

"Couldn't you tell me about that name: *Eadwacer*—however it's said. It was all written down in that book you found and I want to know what it means, and who it was, and why it's ended up here in the house."

" 'Wulf and Eadwacer,' " you mean? I can try, though I don't remember it well, and never understood it even when I did. Nobody ever really knew what it meant, or who they were, only that it's a very sad story that didn't end well."

She turned a little, drowsing against the pillow: "I don't mind, it'll be easier to believe—tell it to me now, just until I sleep."

He moved his foot against the sheets in search of a cooler place, and rested his hand on the white-painted rail of the bed. "A long time ago now, and a long way from here . . ."

"That's not right! Start properly."

He let out a long silent breath. On the wall the remnants of the light from the valve tower faded as the bulb went out. He began again: "Once upon a time there was a woman whose name everyone has forgotten. She lived on an island where nothing grew but heather and no birds sang but ravens and crows. Her hair was the color of grass when it has dried in the sun, and she wore it in two plaits that came over her shoulders, as thick and strong as ropes."

"I've plaited my hair too."

"Yes—but will you listen now? This woman had a husband she loved. It had been raining the day he put his arms around her for the first time, and since then it was the falling of the rain and not the light of the sun that most made her happy. His eyes were like amber and his long hair grew black and gray, and when he hunted beasts or men it was by the light of the moon. Because of this he was known as the wolf, and if ever anyone had known the name he was given at birth, it was long forgotten. Wulf was the name they called him, and Wulf was the name he signed himself. When their son was born, he too had eyes like amber and they called him their wolf pup and their whelp.

"But you see, this was a time of warring, and a day came when the woman's countrymen gave her away as a kind of sacrifice. One night when the crows called from the rooftops and the moon was too young to give any light, she was taken from her Wulf and her whelp to another island, one that lay low among the fens and black marsh grass. The people of this particular island were murderous, and bore long grudges that could only be placated by taking captives and watching them mourn. I think—though I can't be sure—that it was here the man Eadwacer lived, among the woman's captors. Probably he stood where he could not quite be seen, and listened to her singing across the water to the island where her Wulf waited."

The girl stirred, and raised her head a little on the pillow. "But I thought Eadwacer was a woman, too?"

"Not in the tale I'm telling. So can you see it, then? Two islands set apart by a dark sea that froze in winter, and in summer was white with storms. Whenever the rains came the woman remembered Wulf and pined for him so that the bread they brought her was like a stone in her mouth, and the water they gave her was too bitter to swallow. When the rains came she remembered his arms around her, and when there was no rain she thought of nothing at all. Her skin became gray as storm clouds and her hair came out in handfuls, and gathered around her feet where she sat."

If he had hoped to lull the girl to sleep, he had failed. Troubled, she raised herself on a folded arm, and said: "What was Eadwacer doing all this time?"

"It is hard to be certain," said John, "but I think perhaps he watched her as she called over and over to the other island, where Wulf her lover was. In time perhaps they spoke, Eadwacer and the captive woman, and though the captors were his people, and he ought not to have done it, he also put his arms around her, whether or not it was raining."

He could not think where the story went from there, and paused for a while. Beside him the girl leaned back on her pillow and let out a long slow breath. "And how did it end?"

"It never did, only the woman carried on calling to the island across the water, wishing her voice could meet the voice of her Wulf, so they made only one song between them, and whenever she spoke to Eadwacer, though I think he loved her by then, it was with contempt in her voice."

The girl gave a snort of disdain. "I don't like that story—not at all. I don't even know what it means—do you?"

"No, and no one ever has, not in a thousand years." He lifted a strand of her hair from the pillow between them. "But it need not mean anything, I think—it's not necessary to understand everything. Only you should feel what the woman felt, and hear her calling as if we were on one island and she on the other—now go to sleep, won't you, for an hour or two. It's only just dawn, and I'm tired, and I can't think anymore."

She turned obediently away from him and toward the window, where the light was sharpening in the split between the curtains. From underneath them a rumble had begun, that rattled the bed's iron frame against the wall and receded in a while to an insistent whine. Downstairs in the kitchen Hester was washing her clothes.

Tuesday

John sat alone in the garden a moment past midnight, his back against a copper beech, an empty bottle in his lap. A black cloud drew across the sky: it reached the moon and for a moment was fringed in silver; then it moved on, and nothing broke the darkness from end to end.

He was the last to go inside. Behind him, in bright-lit rooms that cast panels of light on the lawn, Hester and her guests sat dozing in armchairs, or listlessly picking at fragments of food. All night they'd moved between the house and garden, alone or pressed so close together their limbs could hardly be distinguished as they danced and drank. Anyone watching would have thought they were fragments of a larger party having a better time.

―――――――

They'd gathered in the dining room at eight o'clock, when Hester struck a gong three times. John—who'd cut himself shaving and stood stroking the tender spot anxiously, wondering if anyone would remark on his newly naked face—had been first to obey the summons. He'd found, among the other man's possessions, black trousers free from stains or cigarette burns, and a dark shirt that only lacked one button. When the others arrived, tricked out in bright dresses and shirts, he felt drab in their company, and stood quietly by the folds of the heavy curtains.

"And where's our Hester gone?" said Elijah, seeking him out and passing him a glass of wine. "Making an entrance, I expect. Have you a gift for her? I haven't—she forbade it—but then women always do, don't they, and one never knows . . ."

"Seen the sky tonight, John?" Clare, appearing at his shoulder, patted his bare cheek and smiled approval. She had found in a cupboard somewhere a white dress with a short skirt that stood out in folds at her waist—it looked rather like a child's Sunday school dress and displayed a grass stain on her knee, and above it her flawless face looked more incongruous than ever. "Have you been outside, and seen it? The sky's getting dark, and it's going to rain . . ."

"I thought I heard thunder earlier," said John, and stooped to kiss the girl's cheek, but she turned away—Hester had arrived, and paused in the doorway, one hand on her hip and the other braced against the frame in a parody of a model's pose. She wore a dress in fine black fabric printed all over with a pattern like the bark of a tree. It covered her from her wrists to her ankles, and over it she had put on a collar of Egyptian scarab beetles carved from bone and stained unevenly turquoise. From a distance it looked to John as if they might at any moment detach from their binding and scuttle to the four corners of the room. Then the guests called out: "Hester, it's Hester . . . for she's a jolly good fellow!" and she made a deep, mannered curtsey, as though her performance had already been made.

John had last seen her early that morning, as she stopped him in the kitchen and drew him into the corner: "That letter—I hate thinking of it, never mind saying it aloud: how could I have been so stupid—did it come? Did you see it? And how can I thank you, John . . ."

"I watched all day," he'd said untruthfully, hoping she wouldn't see in his face the memory of the hour or so at the piano with Eve, "and it didn't come. It's going to be all right—look." And they had both turned to the window, where they'd seen Alex on the lawn with

Walker, struggling with a film projector toppling on iron legs.

As she stood in the doorway taking her applause, John thought she gave him a look of apology and thanks, and he nodded—*might the danger have passed*, he thought, watching Alex fill his glass for the second time and raise it in a general salute.

"And so say all of us!" cried Eve, then dashed to the door and kissed Hester's hands and cheek. "When shall we sing for you, darling? Shall we do it now, and get it over with?"

John, who'd only ever seen her in the boy's clothes that left her limbs bare, had turned away from the door when she came in, wrapped in a green dress with a high upturned collar and thin shining fabric that showed the bones of her hips and shoulders. On her left wrist, positioned precisely above a purplish circle of bruising, was a silver snake consuming its tail. With her curls pinned back from her face she looked to John like a black flower blooming on a frail stem.

Walker wore trousers with a narrow satin ribbon at the seam, and a pleated white dress shirt unbuttoned at the neck. He looked carefully disheveled, as if he'd not yet slept after a grander party elsewhere. Appearing at John's elbow with a glass of wine, he said, "I

put an ice cube in to keep it cold. Drink up, I would—
this could go on for hours." And he drew on a cigarette, narrowing his eyes at Eve, who lifted her hands
to conduct them all in singing "Happy Birthday."

"Happy *birth*day, dear *Hes*ter!" sang Elijah, in a
sober jacket better suited to the pulpit. He slipped into
a bass harmony that so delighted Hester they sang twice
more, while Clare, her hair in plaits, grew increasingly
out of tune and lightly touched John's cheek again. "I'm
glad you did it. Have you hurt yourself? Only—you look
a bit like *him* now," she said, nodding at Walker, who
raised an eyebrow and flicked the butt of his cigarette
onto the terrace.

Later they went into the music room, where the lilies gave off a rank scent that wouldn't be covered with
the perfume Eve sprayed in the air. "I can bear it if you
can," said Hester, sinking onto a threadbare couch and
arranging the beetles at her breast. "We can't have a
party without music." The raised lid of the piano had
been polished; reflected on its black surface, the garden was already at midnight. Eve took Elijah's hand
and pulled him smilingly toward the stool. "Sing what
you like," she said. "I'll find you."

Walker rested his heels on a table, then removed them
under Hester's glare, and murmured to John: "Pass me
the whiskey, would you? I can't take this sober."

The preacher straightened his tie, and with a quick downward glance at Eve as she settled at the keys began to sing. After the first deep melancholy notes had shivered in the floorboards and in the high back of the oak chair where John sat, the woman joined him, fixing her eyes on his: "*As pants the hart for cooling streams when heated in the chase,*" sang Elijah, his eyes fixed on the floor and the lamps putting red lights in his hair. John closed his eyes and saw the deer panicked in a thicket somewhere, thirsty and frightened, and felt his own mouth dry up in the heat. Outside a chorus of crickets started up in the long grass.

The song faded as the preacher forgot the words, and Eve, laughing, ended on a low chord that seemed unfitting to the melody. "Beautiful," said Hester, "but much too sad for me—Eve, play us something merrier or we'll not have the stomach to eat." Elijah inclined his head with a rueful smile, and came to sit in the small space beside her on the couch; she mimed a scowl of disapproval and tucked a cushion behind his head, leaning forward to whisper something that made him smile.

Eve pressed her hands into the small of her back, arching it with a moan that rang loudly under the high ceiling, then launched without warning into a high-stepping tune that made the room a speakeasy and filled all their glasses with gin.

Clare said, "Surely we should dance—who'll dance with me?" but they were too weary with heat, and contented themselves with rapping their heels on the floor, and when the song finished called for another.

"No more from me—everyone has to do something, that's what we agreed." Eve stood, showing a black blade of sweat in the center of her narrow back. "Alex, come on, what have you got to show us?" He stood reluctantly, pulled by Eve at one arm and Clare at another. Finding a basket of fruit on a sideboard, he juggled with oranges, tilting back his head to watch them, grinning at their applause when he snatched another and another, until half a dozen circled at the end of his outstretched hands. John felt pricked with unease: *they can't really be fooled by all this*, can they? he thought, watching the young man nail up a smile.

Then one of the open windows slipped its latch and blew back against the wall. It startled Alex, who dropped the oranges and watched them roll between the legs of chairs and tables. One burst as it struck the bare floor and filled up the room with its Spanish scent.

"Was that the wind?" said Eve, running to the window and leaning out. "It's getting colder—look at my arms: I have goosebumps." She thrust her arm toward them, and John saw the fine dark hairs raised in the sudden chill. "The storm must be coming, after all," she said. "Come on, let's go outside, let's go out and wait for the rain."

"A tenner to whoever feels the first drop," said Walker, following Eve into the garden with his hand at the back of her neck.

The hum of crickets in the long grass rose and receded like a dry tide, and the wind picked up dust from the lawn. Hester clapped with feigned surprise when she saw they'd brought out a white sheet and stretched it between a pair of poplar trees. "Dear me," she said, "what on earth have you been planning?" On the terrace the film projector rested against the sundial.

"Sit down there, sit down," said Walker impatiently, stooping over the projector and fiddling with a case of film pock-marked with rust. Sighing they all subsided onto blankets and cushions brought down from the bedrooms, glancing behind to wave at Elijah, who'd brought his chair to the long windows beside the patio and raised his glass in reply.

Clare leaned against John's shoulder. "I thought I felt a drop of rain but it's just me, I'm sweating, look," and she turned her face up to show him.

The breeze had moved on elsewhere, leaving the air so thick with moisture they felt the weight of it on their shoulders. The bright-lit bank of the reservoir wall seemed to have crept closer while they were inside, and behind it the black fringes of the Thetford pines were unmoving against the sky. Hester let out a moan as she sank onto a cushion: "I wish the dam would break, I wish it would, and float me away"—then glanced guiltily first at John and then at Alex, who seemed not to have heard and was wetting Eve's feet with a watering can.

"There," said Walker, rubbing dust from his hands. "Do you remember this?" The reel of film began to tick through the projector, and Hester appeared as a girl. Forty years were crossed at the push of a switch: the same black eyes challenged the camera from the same face, a little softer perhaps, and framed by thick black hair that fell over her shoulders. The sound was cracked and faint, and the rising wind tugged at the sheet and distorted her features. They watched in silence, glancing curiously over at the woman seeing her youth replayed in front of her. The young Hester raised her arms above her head—*What am I saying? Have I lost my senses?*—then the sound hissed and cut out abruptly, and she was left silently mouthing at them.

"Turn it off, turn it off," cried Hester, delighted. "And I can still remember the lines, you know: *At every word I say, my hair stands up with horror!* Racine, of course," she said to John, as though confiding in a fellow conspirator, and he nodded, though he'd never heard the words.

Walker took out the reel of film and handed it to Hester, who idly began pulling it from its case. "I don't remember having ever been so young," she said, winding the tape around her fingers: "But at the same time, I don't think I've ever grown older . . ."

Eve sank onto a rug beside John, thoughtfully running a thumb over the bruise on her wrist. Seeing it, John flushed with shame and confusion—how could he have hurt her; no one else would have done it; he must lack something essential, after all . . . She caught his eye and shrugged, smiling, and it was so like the acceptance of an apology he hadn't yet managed to give that his throat constricted, and he bent forward to say with hurried relief, "It was dreadful though, wasn't it? She couldn't act at all!"

She grinned, and put a finger to her lips, then turning to look over her shoulder called out, "Cake, Clare—time for cake!" and the other girl dashed indoors and reappeared carrying a uneven white-iced confection on a peeling silver board.

"No candles, thank God . . . ," said Hester.

"There wouldn't have been room," said Walker, ducking a blow to his ear then catching her hand and kissing the knuckles one by one.

"But we can sing again, can't we?" Clare looked anxiously at John, who found himself leading another chorus of "Happy Birthday" as Alex thrust up his glass and made an arc of red wine in the air, and Elijah joined in from across the terrace.

"Someone else cut it, my hands are full," said Hester, showing them a tangle of film on which her face in miniature was repeated every inch. There was a quiet snap, and the wind tore the sheet from the pegs tethering it to the branches, and blew it onto the patio where it huddled in the corner.

"Give me the knife," said Walker, cutting savagely into the cake. "I'm hungry." It split open, and the smell of almonds mixed with spilled wine and the herby scent of the parched grass. "Oh, it could be cyanide in there," he said. "We'll all be found dead in our beds . . ."

Eve smilingly pushed the first piece between his open lips. "No more than we deserve," she said. "Hester? Will you risk it?"

John had stood then to ease the aching in his legs and wandered away toward the reservoir. A column of cloud struck a barrier and began to spread outward in the shape of an anvil showing clearly on the darker sky behind, and against the wall poppy seeds rattled in their husks. He saw the uneven swing hanging from the poplar tree, stirring in the rising wind, and sat there watching for the storm, listening all the while . . .

". . . and who was that new young man, Hester, with the shaving cut and the dark shirt? You never said you'd invited strangers in . . ."

"I forgot the words, forgot them! I used to remember every hymn in the book, you know—all the verses—no I'll stay here, I'd rather stay indoors . . ."

". . . so handsome, and so tall, but has anyone seen John tonight?" That was Eve, laughing—did she know her voice carried to him over the lawn?

"Are we out of wine? We can't be. Give me that bottle, let me see . . ."

"I didn't go down there today, I was sleeping. There was a letter, you know, and I took it upstairs to read then lay down on the bed and went straight off, went out like a light—maybe I'll go down later and check, just once before the rain starts. Will you come? Who'll come with me?"

"One afternoon, yesterday I think it was, it was so hot I heard the paint blister on the windowsill."

"I was reading on the lawn today and I swear a fly just died in the air and landed on my lap."

". . . *dark, dark hath been the midnight* . . ."

"Elijah darling, I wish you'd stop. It's my birthday after all—were there never any happy hymns?"

". . . *glory, glory dwelleth in Immanuel's land* . . ."

"Eve, give him something to drink."

"Did you see that? Look east—no, over there, past the trees—lightning, definitely, down on the horizon . . ."

"And it's colder, I'm sure. Let me have your jacket, Walker, my shoulders will ache . . ."

"Play a game with me, Evie, the ones from when we were little"—and with the smack of palm on palm:

"*I gave my love an apple, I gave my love a pear,*
I gave my love a kiss on the lips
And threw him down the stairs . . ."

"It's going to rain! Did you feel that? It's going to rain!"

". . . *après moi, le déluge* . . ."

"But surely it would have to rain for forty days and forty nights to break the dam, even if he was right all along?"

"Don't talk about it, not on my birthday, I don't want to hear it. And look how happy he is, dancing with Clare, look how alike they are . . ."

". . . is that an owl?"

"It's the wind."

Much later Clare came to find him, her hair coming out of its braids and her skirt streaked with dust. He was sitting cross-legged on the lawn, an empty bottle leaning on his knee, plucking stems of grass and winding them around his thumb. "There you are, I've been

looking and looking. Hester says we should go inside—
the rain will start soon, and I saw lightning, twice, over
there." She pointed toward the reservoir—it was coming closer.

"I want to stay here a while longer," said John, "and
watch it coming."

"Can I sit with you? Look—Alex gave me this." She
sat beside him, reaching into the bodice of her dress
and taking out an envelope. John dully recognized the
careful handwriting on the front, the name *ALEXAN-
DER*, the unfranked stamp. So it had come after all,
while he'd been sitting with Eve, or while he'd raged
about the garden afterward like a petulant child, still
feeling her wrist in the circle of his fingers. It had been
such a small thing to ask him to do, and he'd failed,
even at that.

He said, "What's inside?"

"I didn't look! You can't open someone else's
post—didn't your mother tell you?" She picked up the
bottle and turned it upside down. A trickle of wine fell
onto the grass. "He told me to get rid of it. He said he
didn't need it anymore. Shall we burn it?"

"I don't have any matches," said John.

"Oh." She turned the envelope over and over in her
hands. "Shall I go and get Walker? He always has some,
and he always knows what to do . . ."

"No," said John, too quickly, and she looked at him in surprise, turning the envelope in her hands. Then she said, "Then I'll bury it," and began to scratch a shallow trench in the dust. Then she put the folded paper in the hollow, and he helped her cover it over and find a stone to weigh it down.

"I bet we'll never know who sent them," she said, patting the stone three times. "But I think it must have been someone wicked, though Elijah says there's no such thing, and we're all as bad as each other . . . if I ever found them out I'd find a way to hurt them, you know." She gripped her hands together until the knuckles whitened, and her face, when she turned to look at him, was suddenly not childlike at all, but set hard with fury.

"Maybe they did it because they were unhappy," he said, and she shook her head.

"No, just bad, I think."

"How is he? How has he been—did he read the letter, then?"

"Oh yes, he must have—but he's fine: they don't hurt him anymore. Nothing seems to, not even that woman by the sea and the boy who hurt himself. He's all right. He'll be all right." She dusted her hands on her dress. "Can we go now, John? Let's go inside. I didn't put my shoes on, and my feet are cold—and what if the storm comes and we're still here, sitting under a tree? The lightning will get us!"

She pulled him to his feet, her arms far stronger than he'd thought they'd be, and they picked their way through empty bottles and a plate that had been broken when Hester, heavy with wine and heat, stumbled indoors. Someone had brought out the book of poems with its white vellum cover, and it lay open at "Wulf and Eadwacer." John bent to close it, and would have put it in his pocket if Clare hadn't dragged him on: "Can you feel it coming? The air's fizzing, and it's making my head hurt."

He stood with her at the music room window watching the storm clouds pile up above the reservoir. The wind moaned through cracks in the window frame, and the gray air drew a veil over the garden. It was quiet indoors, and from somewhere along the corridor someone was talking in a low murmur. It might have been any of them, and John strained to hear better, wondering if it was Eve.

It won't be long now, he thought, and wanting again to gather everything he saw to be kept safe and complete in memory, gazed steadily around the room as though it were the face of a friend leaving for another country. The curtains at the window were torn and speckled with damp, and as he watched, a flake of plaster detached itself from the ceiling and floated down like a leaf on a still day. Beside him Clare scratched the paint on the windowsill with her thumbnail, and leaned her head on his shoulder. She said, "You don't think he was right all along, do you?"

John bent his head, and let his cheek rest briefly against the top of her head. Her hair was warm, as though it had soaked up the last of the sun.

"He wasn't really in his right mind, I think. No, he was wrong—we're safe here." She sighed, and her head grew heavy on his shoulder. After a while he thought she must be dozing where she stood; but then she straightened with a cry of delight, and leaned forward to push the window open. A gust of wind threw it back against the wall and cracked the glass, but they neither heard nor saw—it was raining at last. Amazed, they put out their hands to catch cold water in their palms; then all at once there was a change of air so sudden they felt it deep in the channels of their ears. Clare shivered, and began to step away from the window into the darkening room. "Don't let the rain blow in," she said—then arrested by something she'd seen began to point down toward the garden. "Oh—John, what's that? What's happening?"

A flock of small white birds was flying down toward the reservoir, and John leaned out to see better and to hear their song; but it was only sheets of paper carried on the rising wind.

"What is it? Where is it coming from?" On the terrace the girl knelt to pick up a sheet of paper from where it had been pinned to the stones by the rain, and her white dress darkened at the hem. Water streamed over her hair and into her eyes, and she held up the paper, laughing and calling to John, beckoning to him to come out. He began to feel cold and uneasy—he wanted to turn his back on the darkening garden, and wait out the storm in his bed upstairs with the windows fastened against the sky.

"Come out, John—why aren't you coming out? Look, it's only Elijah!"

Turning his collar up against the sudden chill, John went out onto the wet stones and turned to look at the house. All the windows were lit, their curtains drawn back, and directly above them, framed in a panel of light, Elijah stood with the naked lightbulb swaying in the wind and sending his shadow back and forth across the wall. He'd opened the windows as far as they'd go, and held sheaves of paper in each hand which he threw out onto the wet wind. Currents of air lifted them briefly toward the eaves of the house, then they were tossed down on the garden, where the light from the tower was hazy with rain.

"Elijah!" Clare called, waving the paper she'd picked up like a handkerchief. "Can you see us? What is it? What are you doing?"

He heard her, and waved to them both; then, laughing, began to throw out handfuls of paper until the air was full of it.

Then the first lightning strike came, a bluish filament leaping from cloud to cloud, and the whole house sprang out from the darkness then receded into the rain. The full-bellied clouds bore down upon the roof, and John thought: *Just another few feet and we'll all be swallowed up.* Turning his face into the rain, he shouted to the preacher, "The sky's falling in, Elijah— you were right all along!"

"You know, I don't think I've ever seen him laugh," said Clare, but he couldn't hear above the noise of the rain on the stones and the slate tiles of the roof.

When the second lightning strike came it seemed to John that the light came from inside the earth, was an upward surge that shone out through the windows of the house and every crack in the lawn and every fissure and borehole in the trunks of the trees receding into the rain. It gave the world a moment of absolute clarity, and in it the preacher at his window saw something that made him rigid with terror and warning; even above the hammering of the rain they heard his frantic bellow.

John looked down at the water at his feet and thought: *so he was right, after all—the dam has broken.* But no, that was absurd: it was only the rain pooling on the terrace stones, rising, having nowhere to go. Elijah shouted again, gripping the windowsill and leaning so far out that John was afraid he might fall, and he put out his arms as though that would be enough to catch him.

Clare said, "What is it? What's happening?" and gripped John's arm so hard above the elbow that a few days later he found a mark, and was grateful for a reminder that he had been there at all.

"I don't know, I can't hear . . ." Elijah vanished from the window, and all they saw was the shadow of a moth beating against the light. John wanted to call out for the others—none of this was anything to do with him; he ought not to have been there at all; surely someone else was coming? In the high wind a tile slipped free from the greenhouse roof and shattered, its shards lost in the rising water, while beside him Clare plucked frantically at his shirt. Then away to their left, as the lightning flared again, he heard a door slam from the side of the house nearest the garden wall. A moment later Elijah, his head lowered like a charging bull, ran down the garden toward the reservoir at the end. It was then that John realized it was not, of course, the dam breaking: it would have come not in a rising flood but a rush of black water. But whatever Elijah had seen had made him forget his fear of a godless earth, and was a nearer and more urgent danger, and John began running too, grasping for the young woman's hand.

The lawn was too dry to suck up the rain, which might as well have fallen on a tiled floor, and as they ran, water dark with mud and leaves lapped at their ankles, and the white-covered book was open again, floating facedown in the reflection of the swing. Ahead of them the bright grass verge of the reservoir wall was an indistinct barrier, and above it the yellow light from the tower showed clearly.

It wasn't until there was another lightning flash, a bright thread connecting two black banks of cloud, that John saw what Elijah had seen from his window: Alex, standing at the farthest edge of the verge beside the reservoir, staring fixedly down at the water. Below him on the rubble beach the lapping water had begun its rise toward the rim of the embankment. As they watched he tilted back his head as though seeing perforations where the rain came through, and the water dragged his shirt from his back. On they ran, calling out his name; he stepped once toward the water and in his arms they saw a black object, small and heavy. The unkind light came again and lit each separate cloud, and John saw Hester in her party dress, beetles scuttling at her throat, rise up the embankment behind them. Her wide eyes were rimmed in white; she stumbled and slipped, and might have fallen if Walker and Eve hadn't appeared at her side and taken her weight between them. On the surface of the rising reservoir, the water moved in eddies as though just beneath large fish waited patiently, and the pines at the water's edge let loose a volley of cones as the rain struck their branches.

Alex raised his head—he'd heard his name—and John saw it was the cannonball he held, so heavy it raised the tendons in his neck. He moved toward the curved steel barrier marking the place where the reservoir grew deep, and stood gazing fixedly downward. It occurred to John that perhaps he was looking for the post office sign; he shouted out idiotically, "No, it's not there, it's this side, it's over here!" The wind threw his words elsewhere, and Alex never heard—without looking back, he stepped over the barrier and into the black water rising, which snatched at him as though it had been waiting all along.

Clare covered her face with her hands and shook her head violently, as though she refused to believe what she'd seen. Beside her Hester first sank to her knees then began to scrabble at the grass to get enough purchase to stand again; she was not crying, only saying, "No, no, not him, not now," on a rising cadence that died down for a moment, then started up again each time she drew a breath.

John pulled his arm from Clare's grasp and tried to run forward, tugging at the neck of his shirt, but there seemed no strength in his legs, which buckled beneath his weight before he could reach the water's edge. By then Walker had stripped and with a face set in courage or denial jumped into the reservoir. Eve, her curls drawn into a glossy cap, leaned over the barrier, calling the names of the two men in turn as if she might be able to coax them out of the water, while beside her Elijah clasped his hands under his chin, his eyes closed and his mouth moving.

"Too late for that, isn't it?" said John, fear making him unkind, and he stood with Eve at the barrier, staring into the black water. Later he would think of those minutes as having been hours of waiting—he and the preacher poised at the water's edge, uncertain how to help, Eve trembling between them, Hester digging at the grass while Clare bent over her, trying to lift her coils of hair out of the mud. But it could only have been less than a minute before Walker plunged upward through the water; he gulped at the air then was gone for a moment, returning with a dark head cradled in the crook of his arm. He called out, struggling against violent currents; John, his weight borne on Elijah's shoulder, leaned over the barrier with hands outstretched, shouting encouragement as though it had been just a race all along and there might still be a winner—"That's it, Walker, come on, that's it, only a little farther."

Then the young man was slipping in their hands, his forearms grazed by the cannonball, wet and cold as one born underwater. Walker, his back bruised by the concrete of the reservoir wall, clambered over the barrier and shouted to Eve as if she were at the other end of the garden, and not at his side trying to cover his shoulders with a soaking shirt: "Run—you're fastest—call for help: tell them we tried . . ."

Clare went slowly to her brother, moving her head from side to side as though disbelief might make the whole evening a lie. The boy lay on the bank with his arms above his head. Blood ran from a shallow cut on his forehead and mingled with the rain so that a pale stain began to spread over his breast. She picked up Walker's shirt from where he'd dropped it in the mud, and began to dab at the cut, saying, "He'll be cold, won't he? He'll be cold. He mustn't get cold because it always goes to his chest."

Elijah started as though he'd remembered something—"Oh yes, a blanket, that's it"—and ran down the slope toward the house. Hester had fallen forward onto all fours, her head hanging low until her forehead pressed into the mud, the blue beetles scattered over the verge. Now and then she dabbled in the wet grass as though she were trying to reach him, but the rain dragged at the heavy folds of her dress and weighed her down.

John knelt beside the boy. Remembering a long-ago lesson in a school hall, he tilted his head, cradling it gently between his hands, and was surprised to find himself murmuring, "I'm sorry—oh, I'm so sorry." As the heavy head tipped back, dirty water spilled from between his lips. John leaned forward and tried to fit his mouth over the boy's, but the rain made his skin slick and most of the breath he gave was lost. Walker knelt beside John, and finding Alex's heart with his hands released his weight onto the boy's white chest, counting under his breath. Clare counted with him, dabbing at her brother's blue-lipped face: "One . . . two . . . three . . . four . . . One . . . two . . . three . . . four . . . we've got you now, John's got you and everything's going to be fine . . ."

Then there was a new kind of lightning, fitful and blue at the end of the garden, and as the rain began to recede John lifted his head from the boy's and saw it wasn't the storm but an ambulance, and Eve running with her long skirts raised, two men running behind.

Much later John sat on the edge of his bed in his own shirt, the collar an unaccustomed pressure on his throat, the buttons too tight at the wrist. The tower light had gone out and a mild sun was rising, but now and then he shivered with a sudden chill. The borrowed clothes were wet, and he hung them out to dry, putting the glass eye back in its pocket—*Sorry, sorry*—and patting it twice. He opened bags and boxes and returned the other man's treasures—the little severed limbs, the stolen books—running his thumb over the labels with their familiar name. The painted Puritan wouldn't meet his eye; the child's desk had diminished overnight; the chair could never have taken his weight. Taking the notebook from its drawer, he turned to where the account ended and pressed a hand to the empty page. It seemed so long ago, that hesitant knocking on his bedroom door, that the pages ought really to have crumbled in his fingers. He put the book beside him on the bed and listened: downstairs in the kitchen a kettle screamed on the hob.

They'd taken Alex away so swiftly it had been hard to believe, standing there in the slackening rain, that he'd ever been there at all. Untroubled men in bright coats had carried him on a stretcher wrapped in sheets of silver they said would make him warm. They had wanted to take Hester too—"She should have something to calm her," they'd said to John, as if the decision were his. But she'd refused, clinging to Elijah (and had he always been so broad and so tall?), shaking her head, pale mud staining her dress, watching Alex go. As the men picked their way across the lawn they stumbled and an arm with a little shadow on the skin slipped from under the covers, swinging from the side of the stretcher. Clare had cried out: "Should I go with him? I should go, shouldn't I . . ." but remained at John's side.

"I'll go." Walker had stepped forward, tugging at the blanket they'd draped across his shoulders. "Go indoors, all of you. You can't do anything now, it's too late." He stooped to kiss Eve once on her forehead, and followed them down to the waiting ambulance, plucking at a packet of soaked cigarettes and shredding the useless tobacco between his fingers.

John never knew how long Hester stayed up there, Elijah standing with her as the rain receded to the west. Together he and Eve had taken Clare back to the house, both touching her anxiously on the hair or shoulder, murmuring, "Walker is with him—he won't be cold now." John only looked back once, to see Hester in the mud and Elijah on his knees beside her.

At the garden's end the walls of the house were already drying in the early wind, and the sky had begun to prepare for dawn. The two women went upstairs, their arms entwined so tightly he couldn't make out whose hand steadied them on the banister, and whose reached up to smooth Clare's drying hair.

John had passed the remains of the night pacing back and forth, seeing the upturned face in the rain: had Walker pressed his heart back into beating? Had it been a breath he felt as he'd stooped over him, or was it just the wind?

He took up the notebook again to write a final phrase, but found his pen was dry. Then he stood, making a gesture of farewell at the Puritan and the distant tower, and went out, closing the door behind him. Alone in the hall downstairs he heard Hester weeping, and voices falling silent as they exhausted their store of comfort. For a long while he waited, turning his face to the wall and resting his forehead against the peeling paper, rolling the notebook between his hands—he had every right to join them, and none at all. *So this is also loneliness,* he thought, and felt the painful drawing in his stomach set up again. He was ashamed to find it was Eve who most clearly entered his mind, not Clare crying for her brother, or Hester rehearsing her gestures of guilt and grief. He opened up his arms as if he'd seen her there, and when a door was opened and she appeared before him in her green dress he felt no surprise—anyone would have been willed there by so much longing. He looked once at the fine white lines of her face, drawn finer and whiter overnight, and then down at the note-book in his hands.

"It doesn't matter now, but I've been lying to you," he said. It seemed very important that he should tell the truth. "I shouldn't ever have been here. It was all a terrible mistake."

"I know." She said it gravely, with kindness, which hurt far more than anger might. "I wondered, that first night—Elijah had said he was hardly more than a boy—but I never thought it mattered: I was glad to have you here." She touched the bruise on her wrist, and in the kitchen they heard the preacher almost singing. John thought: *He's probably praying*, and took Eve's wrist between his hands. The skin felt chilled, as though her bones were cold—he stroked her with slow and clumsy movements, trying to pass on the warmth he felt for her, but it made her wince, and he let her hand slip from his.

"If only we'd all told the truth, right from the start," said John.

"No one ever has the courage, not really. And besides, who'd believe it?"

"I did my best," he said. "And I tried to understand. But I've been so tired and my head ached, and I've been so confused." He tried to make a gesture that covered it all—the desire and confusion she'd provoked, and the gratitude that once she'd wanted his company.

She said, "So have I—so have we all," and plunging forward kissed his cheek. When she moved away her mouth was wet; she drew in her lip to suck at his tear; she remained so close he could see the blood beating at her throat. His heart began a hopeless brief ascent, and he stooped over her to draw her within his shadow; then she straightened, lifting her chin as though walking into a high wind, and went back to the kitchen.

Through the open door John saw Hester kneeling, her head resting on the table as she traced the place where the name *EADWACER* had been cut into the wood. Beside her Elijah distractedly sang the old song John had recognized, clutching a mug that gave off clouds of steam. Clare had fallen asleep at the table, and her face was calm. John, remembering the weight of her head on the pillow beside his, would have liked to wake her, but the door swung shut and he was left alone.

———————

Outside, the sun illuminated the clouds that massed in the vaulted sky, and kindled the drops of rain still clinging to the grass. Walker was coming up the path, his footsteps sounding loudly on the gravel, his gray head bowed. When he saw John waiting, he paused to finish his cigarette, and the pall of smoke blew upward. Then they stood side by side in the shadow of the pillars and watched a jay spread out its wings to dry.

"He's safe from all that now, at least," he said, turning the packet of cigarettes over and over in his hands.

"There's that, I suppose . . ."

Then, with a quick impulsive touch on John's shoulder, the other man said, "I don't think you could have done anything different, you know—I don't think any of us could."

John nodded, and gestured toward the cool deep recess of the forest. "I'm going home," he said, discovering that he couldn't remember what home looked like, or what might be waiting for him there.

"Perhaps that's best," said Walker, turning wearily to the heavy door behind them. John looked again at the knocker, with the man's hand raised above the iron plate, and thought: *If I'd known what was coming, I'd've wanted it to stone me until I went back the way I'd come.*

"Come with me, if you like," said John, on an impulse born of sudden pity. "Why don't you let me take you home?" Walker looked for a while out toward the forest fringes, as though he saw there a freedom he no longer sought. Then he shrugged, and passed a long-fingered hand across his face. The gunmetal eyes had lost their edge: he looked younger, but weary, like a man come without honor to a battle's end.

"I can't," he said, and from somewhere behind them they heard the familiar steady progression of chords played on the piano. "I've tried before, you see," he said. "Sometimes I think the tide has turned and I'm glad, forgetting that it always comes in again. And besides—wherever I go, there she'll be." He smiled with startling frankness, as though he'd seen in John an equal and companion. "You'll see." He put a hand on John's shoulder and left it there a while, as if there was something else he would have liked to say, then drawing a deep uneven breath went inside. The door closed, and the iron hand knocked its stone twice against the plate.

From somewhere beyond the forest a pillar of smoke was rising. It furled against itself and began to dissipate, then thickened into a plume blowing east. As John watched, pressing a hand to the pain that had set up in his stomach, it resolved into a flock of starlings that scattered and dipped below the horizon.

One by one he said their names aloud as though to leave them there, and went down the gravel path toward the dripping green-lit canopy ahead. The ringing of a single note on the piano receded behind him, then from somewhere in the forest came the sound of small wings beating and the single-minded flock burst up toward the sun. The black plume on the white sky was a line of print, and John went on walking, trying to make it out.

Acknowledgments

I am indebted to Andrew Motion, without whose wisdom I could not have written this book; and to Hannah Westland and Jenny Hewson, for their priceless advice and their belief in me when I had none. Thank you to Robert Hampson, for making me think.

My love and gratitude to my parents, who made me heir to their love of the greatest of all books. To my darling sisters, my second Dad and my friends, all of whom put up with a great deal from me with more kindness and patience than I deserve: thank you. Particular love to Michelle, Ian, Anna M. and Jon, whose friendships have inspired and sustained me so long; and to Stephen, who makes me want to do everything better.

I am grateful to Gladstone's Library for enriching my life, and to the Society of Authors for their generosity. Finally, I am grateful to Emily Berry for her clear gaze and to everyone at Serpent's Tail whose hard work brought this story to the page.

About the Author

SARAH PERRY is the internationally bestselling author of *The Essex Serpent* and *Melmoth*. She lives in England.